CROSSDRESSING
FORCED TO BE A SCHOOLGIRL

JO SANTANA

First published in Great Britain by Miro Books

ISBN 978-1-906320-12-6

Printed and bound in the UK & US

A catalogue record of this book is available from the British Library

Cover design by Miro Books

CROSSDRESSING
FORCED TO BE A SCHOOLGIRL

CONTENTS

CHAPTER 1

I saved the drawings and shut down my machine. Four and a half months work had gone into the plans for a multi-million dollar new wing to be added to our local Boston hospital. Current building estimates were around forty eight million dollars, Jesus H Christ, this was one big project. It was the pinnacle of my career, albeit a short one. Unable to afford college, I took the job at the Bosplan Company while I scraped and saved to raise my college fees. Marrying Ruth had made life difficult, she was a designer for an advertising company here in Boston. It meant paying rent on a reasonable apartment big enough for the two of us, but we scraped through, paid the bills and put aside a little each month to put me through college later on. Ruth was three years older than me and had a collage degree in art and design, she already had a good job. She was due to go out to Italy next month to work on a contract with her Italian subsidiary company.

I picked up my cup of coffee, sipping it while I thought about Italy, the art, the sculpture, the Vatican, Rome, Milan and Venice. Our plan was for me to travel out with her, she was leaving Boston early so that we could enjoy a holiday together before she started work on her new contract in Milan and I came back to Boston to carry on with my job.

I was dreaming, I had no other way of explaining what happened next. I was walking away from my desk when I tripped on a loose cable, one I had meant to tidy away but kept forgetting. I spun around and my coffee went flying, all over my computer CPU. Not a problem normally, but I had the case off to cool the machine, the weather had been hot lately and it tended to overheat without sufficient cooling. I kept meaning to put the case back on, but always forgot. My coffee flew all over the machine, there was a shower of sparks and then it caught fire, flames and smoke pouring out of the machine. I rushed across the office, grabbed a fire extinguisher and pointed it at the flames, pulled the trigger and the foam spurted, putting out the fire, but not before the fire alarm was ringing all over the building. People rushed into the office, including the owner of the company, Russell Simpson.

"Fucking hell, Robert, what the hell are you doing," he shouted angrily.

"Look, I'm sorry, Russell, I just spilt some coffee, no

harm done."

"No? You'd better check, show me the hospital plans you've been working on. If they're not ready this week, we're in trouble."

"No worries, Russell," I said confidently.

I switched the machine on. Nothing. Oh shit.

"The data will be fine on the hard drive, Russell, we just need to put it into another machine."

An hour later, our technician had extracted the hard drive from the burnt machine. It looked like bread looked after it has been in a toaster for at least 45 minutes. Black, smoking and wrecked.

"Mister, you'd better look after the back-up drive, that file is the most important thing in your life at the moment," Russell snarled.

I looked red faced. I felt like shit, like shit that has been run over by a truck.

"Er, Russell, er, the thing is," I trailed off, feeling sick.

"Are you telling me that you've lost the plans? You haven't backed up the hard drive? Four months work and sweet fuck all to show for it? Have I got to face the hospital board and tell them that some half wit has destroyed the plans, put back the whole operation for several months?"

"Well, I can do the job again, maybe three months will get it done, but," I stammered.

He interrupted, his face black with anger.

"Get out. You're fired, don't ask for a reference, you won't get one. And I'll be sending you the bill for the damage and delays you've caused."

"But, Russell," I stammered.

"Out!" he roared, pointing at the door with his finger.

Miserably, I left to go home. With no money and no job.

Ruth took it well, though. "Robert, it's not the end of the world, you'll find another job. I just hope it's sooner rather than later, we'll have trouble keeping finding the rent otherwise."

"I'll get out first thing tomorrow and start looking," I replied. She smiled gratefully. She was a great girl, sexy, too. The slight difference in our ages never seemed to be a problem, she was after all only three years older than me. There was another problem, not only was she older than me, she was taller. At school, they used to call me 'Shorty,' a nickname that I hated. Ruth said she thought that being shorter than her made me seem sexier than taller men. She was 5 feet 8 inches to my 5 feet 4 in my socks. But I was smaller in every way, slightly built, the classic 7 stone weakling. But that was only my outward appearance, in bed there were no complaints. Ruth was everything to me, beautiful, with dark, glossy straight hair, a narrow waist and tits to die for, I liked nothing better than burying my head in them and sucking on her nipples when we screwed. It wasn't just her body, she was a classic beauty, with smooth, even features, she could have been a model, she had even had offers during her short career in advertising. Not that I was ugly, though. Girls said they found me pretty good looking, although some said that I looked a bit 'girly', some of them seemed to want to 'mother' me. They got the quick goodbye. But I wasn't girly looking, I was sure of that. It was a bloody lie, well, partly a lie, maybe I was the spitting image, almost, of my sister Kathy, who was 16, four years younger than me, but I looked like a guy, 100%. Then again, Ruth had said I had slightly feminine features, but she hastily added that they were the kind of features that girls like her tend to fall for in a man, so I was fairly satisfied, although I wasn't entirely sure exactly what she meant.

I spent the next week working on finding another job. On Wednesday I found a book in the bookshop which described the business of spread betting. Mathematics is one of my specialties, in fact I had been known at school as something of a mathj's whizz. I spent all night reading it, it seemed obvious that there was money to be made. On Thursday, I put my first bets down and by that evening had made enough money to treat us to a meal at a local restaurant. It was a glorious evening, Ruth and I dressed up, drinking the best of their vintage wine. When we got home we had a celebratory fuck, it was magnificent, screwing Ruth was an experience. When she was good, she was real good and tonight we felt that we were over our troubles, so that she was at her peak. She was like a love Goddess, touching, stroking, licking, sucking me in places I didn't even know existed. Finally, she climbed on top of me and guided my cock inside her.

"Mm, I love you so much, Robert, fucking you is, well, wonderful."

"Fucking me?" I protested. "I thought I was fucking you?"

"Well, yes, you are, of course. But sometimes, I love to think that I'm with a girl, you know. It's your beautiful good looks, that's not my fault, is it?"

Damn, I'd been cursed all my adult life with my slightly feminine face and skinny, short build. I'd always had plenty of girl friends, though, but now I wondered if they were attracted to me as a man, or because they saw me as somewhat feminine? Ruth hurried to assure me that she saw me as a total guy, nothing less, a guy that she found exceptionally good looking. I could accept that, especially when we were screwing and she was in the hot seat. She bucked and groaned, finally we came at the same time, a glorious rollercoaster as I pushed hard up into her, filling her cunt with my cum. We lay for a few minutes afterwards, unwilling to let the moment go. Then we parted and I lay on my back. She wasn't finished, and licked my cock, almost stirring it back into life, but enough was enough.

"We've had a great day, Ruth. I haven't found a job, true. Well, not exactly, but I've got this spread betting thing down to a fine art. I reckon we're made. A good meal, a good fuck, money around the corner, what more could anyone want?"

"I hope it does go well," she replied, a slightly worried tone in her voice.

"Don't worry, I'm not a math's expert for nothing," I told her joyously. Damn, losing that bloody job drawing boring building extensions was the best thing that had happened to me. I could run my new spread betting operation from anywhere, I pictured Ruth and I sat in a resort, running my betting business from a laptop on a table loaded with cocktails and exotic local food. Then back to our grass hut, fucking our eyeballs out while dusky maidens served us iced drinks.

By the following Thursday, I was broke, worse, I had run up $40,000 in debts to my bookmaker. A disastrous run of bad luck had wiped me out and now they were looking for payment. I had to get a job and start talking to them about regular payments off the debt from my wages. If I ever found a job, I thought, the recession had hit hard and it wasn't going to be easy. I spent all day Friday looking for something, but came home empty handed. During the evening, my sister Kathy arrived. She had managed to get a high school place at one of our best Boston high schools, our parents were going away to South America for several months and she wanted to stay with us until they returned. We were very alike, so much so that we were almost like twins. We were four years apart and different genders, of course, but we had always felt ourselves to be as close as real twins. I was genuinely please to see her, so I put aside my troubles and welcomed her to our home and helped settle her into the spare room. The next morning, Ruth had to work overtime so she left Kathy and me together. That's when the nightmare began.

There was a thunderous knock on the door. Kathy was upstairs putting away her clothes, I was downstairs tidying the back yard. I went to answer the door, the guy that stood there was enormous, like Schwarzenegger's brother but without the good looks, his face was like a sack full of spanners, hard and lumpy.

"Robert Gilmer?" he spat at me.

"Yes," I replied cautiously. "And you are?"

"I represent the man you owe $40,000 to, plus interest. I'm here to collect."

My knees felt weak. I'd heard about this sort of thing, read about it, seen TV episodes, but never expected it to come to my door.

"I'm sorry, you'll have to call back, I don't have it at the moment." I tried to shut the door, but he put a foot in it, a foot big enough to make Yeti footprints.

"You don't understand, Gilmer, do you? You'll pay one way or the other. If you don't have the cash, I'll take it from you. I'll break your arms and your legs, then take that pretty look off of your face. You'll still owe the money, so I suggest you find it from somewhere before it comes to that. You've got until next Tuesday morning, I'll be around to collect, one way or the other."

Then he surprised me by sinking a fist the size of a football into my stomach. I flew backwards and fell to the floor, totally winded by the incredible pain of the blow.

"Tuesday, remember that," he snarled, then slammed

the door shut and left.

I got up and looked around. Kathy was standing at the bottom of the stairs, open mouthed.

"Christ, Robert, what was that all about? Are you in trouble?"

"No, nothing I can't sort out," I replied.

"It didn't look like that to me," she said. "Look, I've got some money, a couple of thousand dollars, I'll give it to you, I can get it on Monday when I go to the bank. I don't have to start my new school until Wednesday."

"Thanks, Sis," I said. "That's really nice, but I'll manage without it."

"Where will you get $40,000 from, Robert?"

So she'd heard the debt collector.

"I don't know, but I'll find it somewhere. Don't worry."

I didn't want to tell Ruth and worry her, but Kathy insisted, she said that my wife had a right to know what was going on as it would affect her too. She was right, that afternoon we sat down and I laid it all out for her.

"So you're telling me that your successful spread betting business has left us $40,000 in debt that we haven't a hope of repaying, and they're going to either collect it on Tuesday or break every bone in your body. Is that correct?"

I nodded. Ruth continued. "As of this moment, we have no money and you have no job and no chance of getting a job. True?"

I nodded again.

"Well, Robert, what the fuck are we going to do?

Thanks to your reckless gambling, we're in deep shit. Right now you're at risk of being severely disabled and disfigured, possibly for life. Do you have any ideas at all as to how you can get us out of this?"

"No, Ruth, I'm sorry."

It was a miserable weekend, Ruth virtually refused to speak to me, other than to answer yes or no when I asked her a question. Kathy was great, she did her best to cheer me up and offer support to Ruth as well, but no matter how I looked at the situation I saw no way out of it. It seemed to me that I had two choices, one was to disappear and go a long way away, and stay away. The other was to wait around to be smashed and beaten to a pulp. Whichever way I looked at it, my life was over, I suspected that Ruth saw it that way as well. As my black mood deepened, even Kathy got fed up and spent more time talking with Ruth, I felt utterly miserable and rejected. By Sunday evening, they had become very close and Ruth was ignoring me. During the evening we had a blazing row and I decided to sleep downstairs on the couch. It was a long, lonely night. I heard Kathy and Ruth get up at different times, presumably to go to the bathroom. I was tempted to try and patch things up but in the end I just lay there visualizing myself in plaster casts in a hospital, or a vagrant on a Mexican street, until finally I dropped off to sleep. Monday morning was terrible, I felt tired and irritable and Ruth was certainly no more inclined to forgive me than she had been over the weekend. I knew that the next day I would be facing either a very severe beating or having to run away, I moped around trying to estimate which of the two choices to take. Ruth and Kathy kept disappearing and I overheard them talking several times, but I couldn't make out what they were saying. We had a quiet lunch, at the end Ruth said something that suggested there may be some hope.

"Robert, Kathy and I have been talking and we think we may have a temporary solution to your problem. The first thing we need to know is what you have decided to do?"

I couldn't look them in the eye, I just mumbled that I would probably have to run away.

"So what you're saying is that you're planning on deserting me, this would be the end of our marriage?"

I looked up at her and said, "Ruth, it's the last thing I want, I love you so much that I would do anything, anything in the world not to have to leave. But if I stay here and get beaten to a pulp I would be no use to you anyway. Surely you don't want to live with a husband in a wheelchair?"

"What if you could stay here and not get beaten to a pulp? What would you be prepared to do to make that happen?"

"I'd do anything, Ruth," I said. "Absolutely anything, but as none of us has the slightest chance of raising $4000, let alone $40,000, it's impossible."

"It's not impossible," Kathy said, speaking for the first time. "Ruth and I have got a plan that we think would work."

"A plan? What exactly do you mean," I said curiously.

"It's quite simple," Ruth said. "Our idea is that we will dress you up in Kathy's clothes and you can stay here, pretending to be her. Kathy's middle name is Maria, so she will become Maria as far as anyone is concerned. Robert, you two look so alike that people will take you to be sisters, even twins."

It was a crazy plan, and I told them how ridiculous it was.

"It would never work," I said. "It's true that my features are very similar to Kathy's, obviously because she's my sister. But the resemblance ends there, I'm not a girl, I don't look like a girl and I don't even want to be a girl. Everyone would know and I would be ridiculed."

"What if people didn't know?" Ruth asked me. "Supposing you were that convincing that everyone did take you to be Kathy?"

I thought about it for a moment, picturing the absurdity of me dressed in my sister's clothes. But before I could say any more, Kathy spoke again, her eyes sparkling.

"Come on, Robert, why don't you give it a try, we'll dress you up and when you see what you look like, you can make up your own mind. It's either that, or your marriage is over. Unless of course, you want to spend the rest of your life as a cripple."

I thought for a moment. I guess there was nothing to lose, at least we could dispose of this ridiculous plan and then work out my next move. I was considering Mexico, but how on earth I would manage to survive without any money I had no idea.

"Okay, I'll try it and you'll see how I look, but I warn you, I'll look ridiculous, like a drag artist."

They seemed to have it all worked out, they dragged me upstairs, chattering excitedly and Ruth helped me to strip off my clothes, down to my shorts.

"We'll need to remove all of your body hair, Robert, girls don't have body hair, you know," she laughed. It was the first time I had heard her happy for several days.

I grumbled a lot, but to be honest I was so demoralized that if she had said I needed to cut my head off I think I would have gone along with it. It would have been a quick end to everything. She found her ladyshave razor, carefully covered me with cream and shaved my legs, chest, my back, arms, even my hands. Not that there was much hair to begin with, I had always been conscious of my lack of body hair and wished I had more to make me look more macho. She plastered hair removal cream all over my face and after a short time ordered me into the shower to wash off. It did feel strange, my whole body was totally smooth, not a trace of hair. Even my face was smoother and if I had looked younger than my true age before, now I looked even younger.

"Right, I'll find you some underwear. Come on into the bedroom." I followed Ruth and she had ready Kathy's spare bra and panties. I stared at them, feeling my face glowing red with embarrassment, but she gave me a stern look that warned me not to argue, fastened the bra over my chest and padded the cups with several pairs of her spare tights, so that I had a pair of firm, youthful tits on display. She handed me the knickers and I stepped into them and pulled them up, realizing that I was stepping into more than just a pair of girls panties, I was stepping into a totally new identity.

"Kathy has been wearing stockings lately, apparently it's all the craze at her last school, the girls say it looks sexy, so she's sorting out a pair of her stockings and a suspender belt for you. We'll go and see what she's got," Ruth said.

My red-faced embarrassment deepened and I argued with her. "For God's sake, Ruth, I can't go into Kathy's room wearing her underwear."

"Don't be so stupid, of course you can. Remember, you're supposed to become Kathy so you'll need to get used to it."

My sister was waiting in her bedroom with a broad smile on her face.

"Gosh, you really look pretty, Robert. My bra and knickers suit you, I thought they would, the pink with the rosebud pattern looks so sweet. Your shape is a little bit too masculine, so I'm lending you my waspy, it's got removeable suspenders to hold up your stockings."

She passed Ruth a garment that looked like a corset, with long suspenders hanging down. Ruth fastened around it my waist, told me to breathe in and then fastened the garment shut, it closed with a long row of hooks and eyes. I let out my breath and was aware that the corset was holding my stomach in tightly, compressing my waistline and making breathing more difficult.

"Jesus, do I have to wear this?" I asked. "It's really uncomfortable."

"Yes, of course you do," Ruth said. "If you're going to be a girl, you need to look like a girl. Besides, we may need to get you a proper corset, to give you some shape, so what you're wearing is nothing compared to the real thing."

She knelt down and pulled my stockings up my smooth legs and showed me how to fasten them to the suspenders. She finished fastening one stocking and made me do the other, it took several minutes for me to get the hang of it but finally I had the stocking securely fastened. They were opaque black, which certainly hid any blemishes on my legs. I had to admit that I looked pretty girly in them my new hosiery.

"What have you got next for our new girl?" Ruth asked.

Kathy pulled hangers out of the wardrobe and showed us.

"The best thing is to try my school uniform, if that looks convincing I reckon it will work. Here, put this on," she said, handing me a short waist petticoat. The waistband was elasticated and I pulled it over my hips. I was amazed, I really did have hips, the waspy had pulled in my waist about three inches and given me what appeared to be a pair of feminine hips. The tiny petticoat sat snugly over my hips.

"This is the standard school uniform blouse, put this on and button it up to the neck," Kathy said to me, handing me a white blouse. It was next to impossible to button it up, women's clothes of course button up on the opposite side to men's, but eventually I managed to do it.

"That looks nice, it fits you really well," she said. "This is the school skirt, put it on."

The skirt was a short, maroon, tartan pleated kilt that fastened over my waistband with two buttons. The blouse was tucked neatly inside and Kathy produced a school blazer in a plain dark red color.

"Before you try on your blazer, perhaps you can get Ruth to do something about your hair and some makeup," she said.

"That's a good idea, come back into our bedroom and I'll see what I can do to your hair and face. Kathy, do you have any shoes for our schoolgirl to wear?"

My sister handed her a pair of black slip-on patent leather shoes, they were a ballet shoe style and I was surprised that they fitted me so well, until I remembered how close my sister and I were in shape and size. I followed Ruth into our bedroom and sat down on the bed while she got to work on me. She pulled a towel over my shoulders so that my white blouse didn't get stained, then pulled my hair out of its ponytail band and got to work with a brush, comb and scissors.

"For God's sake, don't cut my hair," I said to her nervously. "I like to keep it long, the last thing I want is to have it cut short."

"Don't worry," she said. "I'm just shaping it a little to give it some style."

It must have been a complicated style because I sat there for more than half an hour while she fiddled, getting my hair into some kind of shape that would match my new identity. Finally, she was ready and she got out her makeup.

"Kathy," she called to my sister, "could you come in and do her nails, they need something done to them to make them look a little prettier."

Kathy came in with a bottle of nail varnish and made me hold my fingers out while she began painting them. While she was doing it, Ruth worked on my face with a thick foundation that covered my blemishes, not that I had many, then she went to work with blusher, lipstick and eye makeup.

"You won't need false eyelashes, Robert," she said. "You've got lovely feminine eyelashes anyway, I'll just enhance them with some mascara."

"Whatever," I said. I felt totally and utterly ridiculous sitting on my bed wearing my sister's clothes, but I knew I had to carry through this charade so that I could show them how stupid their idea was, then I could get changed, pack a case and head south. At least Ruth wouldn't be able to blame me for not trying.

The two women were chatting away happily while

they transformed me into some semblance of a girl.

"I think she could do with ribbons in those bunches," I heard Kathy say. She? My God, they were talking about me. I wanted to shout out and tell them to stop referring to me as a she, but I decided that it would be best to let them play their little game to the end, I didn't want to appear ungrateful, they were only trying to help me after all.

"Right, get up, put your blazer on and let's see how you look," Ruth commanded.

I stood up, pulled on the dark red blazer and stood waiting.

"Jesus Christ," Ruth gasped. "It's you, Kathy."

"You're right," she said. "It's like I've suddenly acquired a twin sister. Go and take a look in the mirror."

I walked over to our wardrobe and looked at myself in the full length mirror. Or rather, I stood looking at Kathy, in her school uniform. Long hair, held up with dark red ribbons, with two braids hanging down the front, one either side of her pretty, made-up girly face. Smart school uniform, two perky tits pressing the blouse and jacket into just the right shape. The short, tartan skirt, black stockings and ballet style shoes in patent black leather. Surely not, no, I looked around.

"What is this, Kathy, what," but I realized it was me, staring wildly, mouth open.

The two girls smiled triumphantly. "What did I tell you?" Kathy said.

"Kathy, welcome to our home. Say hi to Ruth and

Maria."

What did they call me? Kathy? I looked again at the mirror and then at the two smiling women. I was totally lost for words, what could I say? They had been right and I had been wrong.

"Okay, I agree, I do look the spitting image of Kathy," I said. "But remember, my name is Robert and always will be."

"No, you don't understand." Ruth looked at me intently. "You are Kathy, you don't just look like her, as from this moment on you are Kathy. My name is Ruth, your sister's name is Maria and you are Kathy. Clear?"

I nodded. "Fair enough, I can't argue with that. What's the next step?"

CHAPTER 2

We went downstairs, it felt really strange being dressed in the short skirt and blazer, the school uniform. I spent the next hour being shown how to carry myself like a girl, how to walk like a girl, sit like a girl and even how to talk like a girl.

"Your voice is quite high anyway," Ruth said. "You just need to speak softly and gently and forget all the male macho stuff that you would normally have in your voice. Cut the aggression, speak softly, gently. Try saying 'hi Ruth, hi Maria'."

I could feel my face glowing bright red again, but I did my best, although all I did was send them collapsing into fits of laughter.

"No, no," Kathy said. "You can't speak like that and pretend to be me, here, this is how you do it."

She repeated the phrase again and again and I

practiced until I had it right.

"Yes, that's great, Kathy," she said.

I looked around and then realized that she was talking to me.

"Right, thanks, er, Maria," I replied.

"That's no problem," she said. "Ruth, we need to get Kathy used to walking around and moving like a girl, I suggest we go into town and look around a bit, do some window shopping, maybe we can get some coffee and show the new girl how it all works."

I was utterly astonished. "You must be mad, you surely can't expect me to go out like this, dressed as a girl."

"Don't be so stupid," Ruth said. "What do you mean, Kathy? You're not just dressed as a girl, you are a girl, so from this moment on, forget that you ever were a guy. Your name is Kathy Gilmer. It's never been anything else. Got it?"

"Well, okay," I said." But for Christ's sake, stay close to me, I feel really vulnerable in these clothes, especially this short skirt."

"That's why we're taking you out," Maria said. "Kathy, what you need to understand is how to manage these things in public. How you would sit down in a restaurant, you need to know how to walk properly, how to keep your knees together and take shorter strides. Remember, you're a girl now, everything you do needs to look utterly convincing. I don't need to remind you of the alternative, do I?"

I shook my head.

"Honestly, Kathy," she continued. "I was really worried about you before, now I know that this is going to work."

I was totally terrified when we walked through the front door and it closed, leaving me shut out of the house and trapped out in the open in my feminine guise. We caught the bus into the centre of the city and strolled around sightseeing and looking in store windows. Then Ruth and Maria delighted in taking the new girl into a variety of women's clothes shops and I was made to look through racks of dresses, skirts, jackets and blouses. Then they led me into the lingerie department of Macy's and I was introduced to dozens of pairs of knickers, bras, matching sets of underwear and related garments, suspender belt's, corsets and petticoats. When they finally decided that my familiarization tour was complete, they sent me to the ladies toilet, making sure to instruct me to sit down when I used the john. It felt totally weird, although as I came out of the cubicle and was washing my hands a couple of women came in and just nodded to me in a friendly manner. I was just another girl. I walked out and joined Ruth and Maria and we went for coffee, we sat at a table chatting about the various rules of how to behave as a girl. We had just finished the coffee when Ruth excused herself and said she had an errand to complete, and would Maria show me around some of the sites in the city centre? We agreed to meet up in Macy's restaurant during the evening. All I wanted to do was go home and hide from the world, but I was being led by the nose and had little choice but to do as they said.

Then the moment came that I had been dreading, we bumped into somebody that had met me before. Or at least, had met Kathy before I became Kathy.

"You, girl," a voice called across to me. "Shouldn't you be in school?"

At first I ignored the voice, but Maria shook my arm and said, "I think she's talking to you, she's your new sports teacher at the school, her name is Miss Johnson." She dropped her voice to a whisper, "you need to tell her that you don't have to start school until tomorrow, make sure you call her Miss Johnson, or just Miss."

Trembling at the knees, I did as Maria told me.

"Very well, Kathy, but make sure you are in school promptly at 8.30 tomorrow morning. I'll see you then."

"Yes, Miss," I replied. She stalked away and I breathed a sigh of relief. "My God, what a dragon," I laughed. "I'm glad that I'm not actually going to your new school, I think I would hate having to deal with the likes of her."

Maria looked at me strangely. "Well, I'm not sure it's exactly going to be like that, but we'll talk to Ruth later on and sort out where you go from here. Kathy." She emphasized my new name. We strolled around the lovely old historic parts of Boston, just two sisters that were out enjoying the sights. Strangely, when I caught sight of our reflection in shop windows as we passed, I realized that we did in fact look just like twin sisters, arm in arm, wandering around the city centre. One girl in school uniform and the other in ordinary clothes. It was a strange feeling and I had to keep giving myself a mental reminder that I was a girl and not a boy, and act accordingly.

We reached the restaurant and sat down to wait for Ruth. Two boys came over to us, to my utter horror one of them said, "Are you two girls on your own, how about we join you?" I shook my head firmly, terrified of the situation I was into but Maria fended them off, saying politely that we were waiting for our boyfriends. That seemed to do the trick, although I felt as if I had been kicked in the stomach. I was terrified. We sat for ten minutes drinking coffee and then Ruth arrived and we ordered some food. We had just started to eat when Ruth and Maria began to lay out their plan to keep me in one piece, that is without having my arms and legs broken or having to hide out in some Mexican slum.

"How are you doing, Kathy?" Ruth asked me. "Have you had any problems?"

I shook my head. "None at all, it's gone very well, everyone just takes me as a girl, and in fact the teacher we met just assumed that I was one of her new girls."

"Well, that's because you are one of her schoolgirls, aren't you?" Ruth said.

"Only for today, Ruth," I replied. "Obviously, tomorrow Kathy will be going to start school."

"Yes of course she will," she said firmly. "But you see, Kathy is you. You will be going to start school tomorrow, nobody else. It's absolutely essential that you do this, its part of your cover, part of your new life as Kathy. Tomorrow you will report to school and just be one of the girls."

I wanted the ground to swallow me up. "You must be mad, how the hell could I do that?"

"You already have," Maria said. "We met Miss Johnson and she assumed that you were Kathy, a new girl who will be starting school tomorrow, so what's the problem? It all looks totally natural."

"Problem? I spluttered. "You know very well what the problem is, there's absolutely no way, no way I'm going to that school as a girl, dressed in this uniform. And that's final."

Ruth and Maria glared at me. Ruth spoke first. "It had better not be final, Kathy. You are in a very serious situation, a situation of your own making. For the time being you will be living as Kathy, why do you think we put all of that work into making you look as good as you do? Or do you want to be turned into a cripple for the rest of your life?"

I shook my head. "No, of course I don't, but,"

"There are no buts," she said. "As a matter of fact, I knew you were going to get cold feet, do you know I've been doing this afternoon?"

I shook my head.

"I went home to sort out your clothes," she said. "I got all of your men's clothes, bundled them up and took them to a charity shop. When you get back, you will find that the only clothes you have to wear areKathy's clothes, your clothes, including your school uniform. And by the way, you look very pretty and it, so you shouldn't feel awkward."

I erupted with anger. "What the hell are you talking about? You got rid my clothes, you must be mad?"

"No, I'm not mad," she said quietly. "And keep your voice down, remember, you're supposed to be a pretty 16-year-old girl, not a macho guy who thinks he can get his way by shouting the loudest. Girls don't shout, they get their way by being subtle, you'd better start learning how it works. Anyway, there's damn all you can do about it, the clothes have gone and from here on in you're Kathy Gilmer and no one else, so you'd better get used to it. By the way, I've put all of Kathy's clothes into the spare room. As a 16-year-old you need to have your own room."

Oh Christ, this was getting worse and worse. "What the hell is Maria going to do?" I asked forcefully.

"I had agreed to share the bedroom with Ruth," Maria said quietly. "It is important, Kathy, that you get used to being a 16-year-old girl, and you can't do that if you're sharing a bedroom with a married woman. It's for the best, believe me."

I did my utmost to argue and reason with them, but they were totally unmoving. We walked to the terminal to catch a bus home and I was fascinated by the sight of the pretty young schoolgirl walking along with two other girls. I could scarcely believe that it was me, but every time I caught sight of the three of us in a store window I became more and more positive about the whole scheme. It could work, except for one thing. How on earth could I manage to keep up the charade in a girl's school? I had visions of myself being unmasked and running from the police as well as from the money lenders. In the end, I just accepted the situation and resolved to do my best. Besides, what choice did have? My clothes were gone, on the one side I had two determined females, on the other an ogre who wanted to put me in a wheelchair.

I found it difficult to sleep on my own in the spare room, now my room, Kathy's room. They had given me a pretty nightie to wear, which felt even more strange, I normally slept with nothing on.

"As a single girl, Kathy, you need to preserve some modesty," they said.

I had been shown how to remove my makeup and brush out my hair. In the morning, I got out of bed and started the process of putting Kathy Gilmer back together again. Ruth had bought me a present the previous day, a new corset. It was a much bigger, firmer garment than the waspy that I had worn the previous day. "You need to create more of a feminine profile, Kathy, this will help you immensely. Stop grumbling, you should be grateful that we're helping you. Breathe in and hold your hands up straight up in the air," she said. I did as she told me and she fastened the laces of the garment very tightly. I tried to breathe out and found that it was impossible.

"Jesus, Ruth, I can't wear this, it's killing me," I said.

"Either get it off me or loosen it off a bit."

"No, it looks fine as it is, don't worry, you'll soon get used to it. If you need to take it off for gym or anything like that, there are hooks and eyes at the front, it'll be a bit of a struggle at first but you'll soon get the hang of it."

Laced into the tight corset she sat me in front of a mirror and gave me a lesson in putting on makeup.

"You'll need to know how to do it, girls always check their makeup and touch it up when they go to the toilet. Make sure you do."

I did my best to apply the lipstick and Ruth said it was a reasonable job. The mascara brush was incredibly fiddly, but my eyelashes looked beautifully long when I had finished and I thought how my face was already taking on a very pretty, girly appearance. Both girls agreed with me. Maria had come in to help and show me how to get into the school uniform garments.

"As for your hair," Ruth said. "the plaits either side of your face will stay in, the hair bows have elastics built into them, you just need to pull them out straight and slip the bunches through the elastics. She clicked on the ribbons, already shaped into bows, and looking in the mirror I could see my part of my hair was pushed up and out in two classic girly bunches, framed by the red ribbon bows with the two plaits falling either side of my face.

"You need to put the rest of your clothes on yourself, Kathy, so that you know how to do it."

I nodded. I was already wearing my knickers and Ruth had padded out the bust of my corset to give me reasonable looking tits. I pulled on my thick black stockings and fastened them to the suspenders, buttoned up my blouse to the neck, stepped into my waist petticoat and then pulled on the tartan miniskirt, which I buttoned around my waist. I slipped on my patent leather ballet shoes, shrugged into my dark red blazer and checked myself in the mirror. It was amazing, even though I had done it all yesterday I could still hardly believe that I was looking at myself. I was Kathy, no doubt about it.

I went downstairs and ate breakfast, although I wasn't very hungry, my stomach was full of butterflies, I was that nervous about the coming day. Maria gave me the details of where I was going, the courses I was due to take and she also gave me her backpack, powder blue, with books and pens in it.

"You'd better have a watch as well, Kathy. I've got a spare one, you can take that."

She handed me the watch, a trendy little pink strap holding a pink plastic watch case. I fastened it to my wrist.

"You haven't done your nail varnish, Kathy. You can't wear anything too tarty to school, but I'll find you something neutral. Don't forget you need to do your nails every morning before you go."

I nodded and she went away and came back a minute later with a bottle of nail varnish.

"You'd better do it yourself. You need the practice, when you've finished you can put the bottle in your backpack and you'll be able to touch up your nails whenever you need to."

I painted the nasty smelling concoction over my nails and held my hands out for a few minutes while they dried. Maria looked at the clock.

"The school bus will be along in about 15 minutes, Kathy. You better make sure you're ready. Have you got everything you need?"

I told her that I hadn't got a clue what I needed, so how could I be sure?

"Look, Kathy, you've been to school before, you must have an idea of what you need. Have you got any money for lunch?"

I shook my head. "Here, you'd better take my coin purse, I've got another one I can use upstairs in my case," she said, handing me a pretty little wallet that matched my pink watch.

"I think that is everything," Ruth said. "Remember, you're just a girl going to school, nothing different to what millions of girls do every day all over the world, so chill out, relax and don't worry. The only thing you've got to worry about is if you don't go through with this and you have to face the alternative. And I don't think that bears thinking about."

They wished me good luck, gave me a peck on the cheek and sent me on my way. With my nerves stretched to breaking point, I walked to the bus pickup point, trying to remember to take short steps, keep my knees together and all of the other aspects of female deportment that Ruth and Maria had shown me. I had my backpack slung on my back and I noticed other girls heading in the same direction, looking exactly the same as me. When I got to the bus stop, there were already three girls waiting there and they greeted me in a friendly manner.

"Hi, I'm Kaylee," a pretty, freckle faced girl said to me, she was about 16 years old, my age, I had to remind myself.

"I'm Kathy," I replied with a small smile, "it's my first day."

"Yes, I didn't think I'd seen you here before. These are Christine and Juanita."

The other girls nodded to me and Kaylee chatted happily for several minutes until the bus came along. When we got on she insisted on sitting next to me, it seemed she had decided to take me under her wing. I had no objections, she was quite frankly extremely attractive, I had to keep reminding myself that she was not talking to me because I was a man. This wasn't a girl trying to pick me up, it was simple girly conversation that I had better learn to do very quickly. I did my best to keep the conversation going, adjusting my voice to be gentle and pitched slightly higher than normal. The other two girls were sat in the seat behind us and we all chatted between us, as if everything was totally normal.

"What about the cheerleaders, Kathy?" Kaylee asked.

"Are you planning to join?"

"The cheerleaders?" I replied, alarmed. "Oh no, no, I'm sure they wouldn't want me."

The three girls all laughed. "I'm sure we all would want you, Kathy," Kaylee said. "All three of us are on the cheerleading team and we are on the lookout for attractive girls to join us right now. Quite honestly, you're exactly the right type. You're pretty, don't argue, you know you are, I'll bet you always have boys coming on to you. And youre fit and slim, exactly what we need. Recruiting the right kind of girl has been difficult lately, we won't take no for an answer, Kathy. I'll talk to Miss Johnson later, I'm sure she'll be keen for you to join us."

"That's really kind," I smiled. Inside, I was quaking. How the hell could I keep up with these athletic young girls in those tiny dresses, prancing and leaping around the sports field? Right at that moment, suicide seemed a better option.

We got to school, it was a co-ed and I had to put up with being ogled and whistled at by several boys. I found the office and handed in my forms to the secretary, a stern faced woman, Miss Wennerstrom. She handed me a thick book.

"This is your copy of the school rules, Kathy. Make sure you read them and don't break any of them. We encourage our girls to be involved in sports, so you should consider joining one of the teams. The cheerleaders are on the lookout for new girls, that could be worthwhile, you should take a look at it."

I found my first class, a history lesson, and introduced myself to the teacher, a Mr. Andrews.

"We're covering European history, Kathy, so try and keep up, if there's anything you don't understand, just ask me after the lesson."

"Yes, Mr. Andrews," I replied. I sat down at a desk and went through the lesson, fortunately it was all stuff that I had covered before when I was in school, so there were no mysteries there. The next lesson was math's, which was my particular interest at school and again I went through without difficulty. I remembered the reason I was here, my inflated opinion of my math's abilities. Maybe I should take more notice in class. When the boys separated to go off for metalwork classes and we girls trooped off to the cookery classroom it was a different story. I put on a long white apron and did my best to put the ingredients together for some kind of a cake, I was totally unsurprised when at the end of the lesson I had a soggy heap of wet mixture.

"You'll have to do better next time, Kathy," the teacher said, a formidable lady named Miss Gray. "We expect our young girls to have a high standard of cookery skills to equip them in later life."

I nearly burst out laughing, it sounded like something from fifty years ago, but I dutifully said, "Yes Miss," took off my apron and went to the canteen for lunch. I sat with my new friends, Kaylee, Christine and Juanita. They spent the whole period doing their best to persuade me to join their cheerleading team and I had to promise to think about it before they would give up on me. I kept remembering to keep my knees together, conscious of the constant attention from passing boys. Then it was an afternoon of more lessons and finally I got on the bus to go home. I couldn't believe that I had managed to do it, although there hadn't been any really serious challenges yet, like a sports lesson, when I would have to mix in a changing room with other girls. Did I just think other girls? I meanmt girls, not other girls, I had to remind myself that I was a guy. That was weird, I had spent my first day in girl's clothes and was already thinking of myself as a girl. I would have to be careful.

I walked in the house and Maria stood there white faced. "What's the matter, Maria, you don't look well?"

I walked in and slammed the door, then I nearly had a heart attack. The debt collector was standing in our lounge, glaring at me with a face like thunder.

"Where is he?" he shouted.

"Who?" I squeaked.

"Robert Gilmer," he snarled. "That bastard owes us $40,000 and I'm here to collect, so tell me where he is hiding."

"I've got no idea," I replied, faint with terror.

"I told him that Robert had run away to Mexico, Kathy, but he said he didn't believe me. Tell him it's true," Maria said.

I looked at the heavy, I'd never seen anyone so large, threatening and ugly as this guy.

"Yes, Robert went to Mexico, he left several days ago.

Why, is he in trouble?" I said.

"Trouble like you wouldn't believe, girly," he replied. He looked me up and down, I could see he was drinking in the sight of a pretty schoolgirl, dressed in her short tartan miniskirt, perky young breasts pushing out through her blouse, pretty hair pushed up in bunches with ribbons. I trembled inside, already I was beginning to think like a girl, I had received dozens of glances that day from boys, though without the explosive, threatening power of that man's expression. Now I knew what girls had to deal with every day of their lives, bastards like this. Of course, some of the boy's admiring glances were welcoming, but some, like the lustful stare I was getting now, were anything but welcome.

"I told the bastard that when I came here I was going to collect payment one way or the other," he snarled. "It looks as if it will have to be the other."

He stared at me, then suddenly grabbed the collar of my blazer in one of his huge hands and threw me to the floor. Marias' eyes widened and then she ran to protect me. The brute simply grabbed her too and forced her to her knees.

"Right, you fucking whores, this is where you make a down payment. He shoved Maria onto the floor, so that she was lying on her back, then he pulled me up to my knees. He planted one huge foot on Maria's stomach so that she couldn't move and unzipped his fly. His cock sprang out, huge, hard and disgusting.

"You can blow me, girly. I've always fancied it from a

schoolgirl in uniform, so I think I'll take this opportunity. Come on, you know how it goes, suck it."

"No, never," I shrieked. "That's disgusting, get out of here or I'll call the police."

He laughed. "You're wasting your time, they won't help you. I'll just tell them that you offered to blow me in part payment for Gilmer's debt."

Then he pinched my nose so that my mouth opened to suck in air, as I breathed in he pulled my head forward and forced his cock all the way into my mouth so it seemed to be forcing itself down my throat, deeper and deeper. I choked, gagged, but managed to calm myself and draw in a little more oxygen.

"Now suck it, give it a good licking, I'll hold you here until you do, so you'd better make it good."

I felt totally desperate, tears were pricking at the corners of my eyes, and I realized that I was experiencing what some girls suffered at some point in their lives. It was called rape. I looked down at Maria who stared back at me from the floor. She was appalled to see me kneeling with this man's huge cock stuck in my mouth, but she was also practical enough to realize that we had no alternative. She gave me a slight nod and I gave in to the inevitable and started to give the disgusting creature what he wanted. I closed my eyes tightly and pretended that I was just in a dream. Then I went to work, using everything I knew about the male anatomy, which of course was a great deal, to do a job on him. I licked around the tip of his penis, feeling him shiver as I did so, but all I got for my efforts was that the increased arousal made him force his cock even deeper into my throat. I licked around the great shaft that was stuck inside of me, then licked again at the tip. I moved my mouth backwards and forwards, eventually settling into a stroking, licking motion that clearly was what he wanted. I prayed for it to end, I was desperate to go away to some far place, far from this brute who was, as far as he knew, raping an innocent schoolgirl. But he did not want it to end, and as much as I used every trick to hurry him along, he used all of his reserves of staying power to keep fucking me for as long as was humanly possible. It seemed machine-like, rocking backwards and forwards, licking around his cock, sucking, stroking, I even put my hands up and gently stroked his testicles, touching the sensitive place underneath that I knew to be very erogenous to men. Finally, he began to reach his climax, his breathing became shorter, then he was panting and shouting with a hoarse voice, then he screamed as he came, ramming his prick even further into my throat so that the squirting streams of semen forced down my throat and into my stomach. Finally he stopped, but still held my mouth over his penis so that I could not escape. Then he had had his fill and he let me go.

CHAPTER 3

I was overcome with emotion and I collapsed on the floor, weeping tears of pain and humiliation. Maria got up to comfort me, she put her arms around me and whispered, "it's all over now, Kathy, don't worry, we'll get you cleaned up, we'll get you over this."

My rapist loomed over us. "Now look here, you fucking whores. That was just a little interest on what Gilmer owes. When you hear from him, tell him that he owes my boss $40,000. I'll keep coming here to collect the interest," he smiled licking his disgusting, fat lips. "But I warn you, if you cause any trouble with the coppers, or he tries to get out of paying, my boss will put out a contract on Gilmer, and I'm not talking about broken arms and legs, you hear?"

We both nodded. "Good," he said. "They always pay, one way or the other. If they don't, we make sure that they never run up any debts in the future." He grinned at us. "Dead men can't borrow money. Got it?"

We nodded again. Satisfied, he strode to the door, walked out and slammed it shut, so hard that I thought the it would smash from the hinges. Without saying a word, Maria took me up to the bathroom and helped me to clean my face. I swilled out my mouth many times but I couldn't seem to rid myself of the filth that had gone in there.

"I'll help you redo your make up, Kathy. You don't want Ruth coming home and seeing you like that."

I shook my head and sat on the side of the bath while she busied herself with my makeup and re-made my face. We went downstairs and tidied up the room after it had been messed up by our encounter with the moneylender. We said nothing to each other about the rape. I didn't know what there was to say, what could I say? I had never felt so trapped in my life, sitting in my girl's clothes, the little miniskirt, I just wanted to change into jeans and a T-shirt and run away forever, but I knew that it would solve nothing. If he came back, he could start on Maria and Ruth, that would be even worse.

"How am I going to get out of this?" I asked Maria, my sister. "We can't have him coming to the house demanding a blow job every time he feels like it. Perhaps we should call the police."

She looked dubious. "It's a possibility, but you would have to present yourself as Kathy, go to the police lab for swabs and so on. Could you do that?"

I said no, I couldn't. I looked like a girl, I even felt like a girl, but it didn't mean that I was anything other than who I was, hiding out in a schoolgirl uniform.

"Should we tell Ruth about it?"

"I don't know, Sis. It may not be a good idea to frighten her."

Sis? Jesus, she was already seeing me as a girly, as her sister.

"I think the best thing is to contact the police and tell them about it, but decline to take it any further. That way, they might warn off that horrible man and keep him away for the time being. I don't know what we'll do when Robert resurfaces."

I shivered. Robert was me, how could I reappear so long as this nightmare continued?

"Anyway," she continued. "We'll keep things as they are for now. I've said I'll go to Italy with Ruth so that we don't waste the air ticket, so you'll be able to keep up your work at school."

"My work? What do you mean?" I said, or rather, I squeaked.

"Your work, of course. You're Kathy Gilmer, enrolled at the school, isn't it your work you're doing, your studies? You can finish up the semester, maybe even the year if things haven't cooled down."

"The year? You expect me to dress like this for a whole year?"

"No, but what else would you do?" she asked. "If you

become Robert again, how will you avoid being crippled or even killed?"

I shook my head, I had no answers. When Ruth came home she greeted me like a younger sister, once again giving me a peck on the cheek. Maria and I had decided to tell her nothing, the following day she promised to go and report the incident to the police. One advantage was that she could claim to be either Maria or Kathy with equal honesty. I was instructed to go to school as normal. Normal? Once again I undressed and put on my pretty nightie and slept in the single bed in my own room, Kathy's room. In the morning, I prepared for school. I explained to Ruth and Maria the problem with possibly having to wear some kind of a gym dress, I didn't mention the cheerleaders, I knew that if I had to wear one of those tiny short dresses I would have to shoot myself or jump off of a bridge. They solved the problem by giving me the waspy with the suspenders to put in my backpack. They showed me how the suspenders could be detached. They also gave me a matching bra, ready padded, so that if I needed to change I could remove my heavy corset and just wear the waspy afterwards and bring the heavy corset home in my backpack. They gave me a pair of long white socks and trainers, white with pink trim, for me to wear if necessary. Then I went to school, praying that I would never need these sports clothes. I went to the first lesson, English language, at the end of the lesson my hopes were firmly dashed. The next period was sports and Miss Johnson singled me out.

"Kathy, I put a cheerleading dress out for you, change into it and let's see you try out for the squad."

I did my utmost to protest and refuse, but she was persistent. I also had to contend with Kaylee and the other two girls who seemed determined to encourage me to join them. I went into the changing room and found a cubicle, then I began to get changed. With extreme difficulty I managed to unlock the fastenings on my heavy corset and remove it. I stuffed the heavy garment into my backpack, my stockings came off and went into the bag as well together with my shoes. Then I pulled on my white socks. I fastened the waspy around my waist, after removing the suspenders, and secured it with the hooks and eyes. It was almost as tight as the corset but was much more suitable to wear under the tiny dress. Finally I pulled on my bra and fastened it and pushed it into position so that I was able to display a youthful pair of boobs. Then with a feeling of doom I pulled on the cheerleading dress. It barely covered my crotch, I guess it ended about 3 inches my genitals. It was such a tiny, flimsy garment that I felt almost naked wearing it. Determined to do my best to carry out this idiocy, I laced up my pink and white trainers and went out to join the squad.

For an hour I jumped up and down, waving pom-poms on the end of sticks in the air and practicing a variety of energetic dance steps. At the end of the hour, I was totally exhausted and soaked in perspiration.

I found a private shower with a lockable door in the changing room and showered myself and dried, then put my school uniform back on. For the first time, I managed to do it quite easily. I felt proud of myself and as I completed touching in my makeup, tidying my hair and straightening the ribbons so that they looked pretty on top of my head, I suddenly relaxed and began to enjoy the masquerade that I was involved in. I picked up my backpack and went to join the other girls for the next lesson and by lunchtime we were chatting away merrily like old friends. There was one extremely dark cloud on my horizon and I fretted to work out a way around it. But then it was as if a fairy godmother heard me and waved her magic wand. Miss Johnson came up to us and said, "girls, I'm trying to form an all girls shooting team. Would any of you be interested?"

"What sort of shooting?" Kaylee asked her.

"Rifle and pistol," she said. "We have the use of a shooting range in the school basement, the cadets used to use it but lately no one has bothered and I think it is time we showed the boys what the girls can do. How about it, do any of you want to try?"

There and then the plan began to form in my mind. I had never fired a gun in my life, but I knew that in order to save myself from being raped by the pig who had attacked me the day before, I would do anything.

"I'd like to give it a try, Ms Johnson," I said.

"That's excellent, Kathy," she smiled. "Anyone else?"

"I'll do it, Kaylee said.

"Very good, that's a good start. Come to my office at the end of the school day and I'll take you down to the shooting range and show you what's involved."

The range was dusty and dim. Miss Johnson put on the overhead lights and spot lamps illuminated the targets at the end. She handed me a pistol, a Smith and Wesson model 22A.

"This fires a .22 round, quite small," she said. "But it's accurate and ideal for target shooting. You need to be careful, girls, these guns can and do kill, in the wrong hands."

"Yes, Miss Johnson," we chorused.

"As for the rifles, take a look at this. It's another Smith and Wesson, the M&P 15-22. It uses the small bullet, although they are a little bigger than the handgun rounds. It's very, very accurate at long ranges, you could even use this to practice for the Olympic Games." She smiled, she was obviously a competition shooting enthusiast.

"May I try the handgun, Miss," I asked shyly.

"Of course you can, Kathy. I'll load the magazine, look, this is how it works."

She snapped the magazine into the gun.

"Put on ear protectors, the noise will be very loud in this enclosed space."

I put on the gadget that looked like a big pair of earphones, but colored yellow. Then I picked up the gun and she showed me how to take off the safety. I aimed at the target, squeezed the trigger and the gun kicked and flashed, the bullet hit the target with a clang as it struck the protective plate behind, and I had fired my first shot.

"Try four more, see how you get on, Kathy. You certainly hit the target with your first shot, "Miss Johnson said enthusiastically.

I fired again, four more times. Each time, I could see the brute's face in front of me and I hit it with my bullets, again and again, seeing him fall, bleeding to the ground.

"May I try the rifle, Miss?" I asked.

"Of course, dear. It's already loaded, try five more shots. Do you know how the bolt works?"

"I've seen it in films, Miss, so I know what to do."

"Good. The safety works exactly the same, you need to lie flat on the ground, aim and fire."

I lay on the ground, careful not to ruck the hem of my miniskirt up. Then I fired a carefully aimed shot into the centre of the target.

"Good shot, Kathy, keep going," the teacher said.

I fired repeatedly, seeing the same face at the end of the shooting range. The brute, collapsing in a spray of blood and shattered flesh. At last, I had found the way out of my problem. I stood up, removed the ear protectors and smoothed down my skirt. Kaylee took the next turn and fired five shots with each weapon, the handgun and the rifle. Then it was Miss Johnson's turn, she fired quickly and expertly. When she recovered her target, we saw that she had scored almost perfectly, every shot had pierced the bull's eye.

"Miss, you must have done this professionally," I gushed.

She smiled. "Not really. At one time I wanted to try out for the Olympic team, but I had other commitments, so it never came to anything. But you girls," she looked at us.

"You could go all the way, if you wanted, even the Olympics if you try hard enough."

I knew how far I wanted to go. It was a vicious, raping thug. Ever since she had mentioned shooting earlier in the day, I had fantasized about killing the brute. I still didn't know his name, so I just called him the thug. It was perfect. A 16 year old schoolgirl in a dinky little tartan skirt and white blouse, how could anyone suspect? I determined there and then to spend my time becoming expert with both handgun and rifle, as well as finding out everything there was to know about my target.

"You seem happier tonight, Kathy," Ruth said. She was sitting on one side of the dining table with Maria, I was sat the other side. Was it my imagination, or were these two becoming closer to each other. Well, I should be pleased, my sister and my, well, Robert's wife, becoming such good friends, it was wonderful. But still, there was something a little deeper than just friendship, but no, I dismissed the idea. How could it be anything more, my sister was no lesbian, neither was Robert's wife? I put the idea out of my mind and determined that I would be happy that they were so friendly.

"Kathy, we thought we would give you a night out on the weekend, we can dress up and go into town, do some drinking and go on to a club and show you some dancing, how do you feel about that?" Ruth said.

"That's a great idea," I replied. Then a thought struck me. "The only problem is, you threw out all of my clothes, and I haven't got anything to wear."

They both looked at me mystified. "But Kathy, you've got clothes in your room and anyway we can always go out on Saturday and get you something new to wear."

I suddenly realized what they meant. "You mean I'm to go out as a girl? I thought you meant that I could go back to being Robert for one night."

"Kathy, don't be so stupid," Ruth said. "You know as well as I do that Robert has gone a long way away, he's not going to be back for a long time. Look, we'll take you out on Saturday and treat you to a new dress, how does that sound?"

"That's great, yes, it would be nice to go out and do something different," I told her. In fact I was beginning to get used to being a girl, I'd never really been partying before in any guise other than that of Robert Gilmer and it seemed strange suggesting that I would be going out as Kathy Gilmer. Of course, I had to get used to it. One thing beginning to worry me, I was starting to enjoy being a pretty 16-year-old girl. People treated me differently and I felt differently too, something inside me seemed more alive when I wore my school uniform with the tartan miniskirt. My friends, Kaylee and the others were really nice to me, I seemed to have the best of all worlds. The only thing I didn't have was Ruth, at least, not as a wife. I really missed her and sometimes felt quite jealous of Maria for sharing a bedroom with her. Still, I just had to get on with it for the time being.

"What kind of a dress?" I asked them.

They smiled broadly and we started chatting about different styles and hem lengths.

They took me back to Macy's and we three girls looked at racks of party dresses. In the end, I chose a little black dress, the hemline was just as short as my school miniskirt and the dress was sleeveless, it felt to me as if I was wearing nothing more than a long T-shirt. My ribs were aching, before we left the house Ruth and Maria had insisted on lacing my corset much tighter so that I would have a more feminine body shape that would look better in a party dress. When they forced the laces really tight I could barely breathe, it hurt, I argued with them, but they insisted that it was necessary if I was to look pretty and sexy. I paraded in front of the mirror in the little black dress, I had to admit that the slim, curvy looking girl that I saw in the mirror looked pretty good. I felt so proud, I completely forgot about the corset, if the tight lacing was necessary to make me look this good I would have to get on with it, it was really worth it.

"Ruth, shouldn't we find Kathy some sexy high heels to go with her new dress?" Maria said.

"Good idea," Ruth said. "Come on girls, let's find the shoe department, Kathy, we'll bring your old clothes, keep the dress on for now and we'll choose some shoes to go with it."

They walked excitedly through the shop until we came to the shoe department. They made me sit down while they went away and chose some shoes for me. I took off my black patent school shoes and waited. Soon, they came back with a selection of wicked looking high-heels, all stiletto's, pointed toes and incredibly sexy. A saleswoman was with them, "I see, you're buying a pair for this young lady. Did you want very high heels or something a little lower?"

"Ruth, Kathy should wear something really high and sexy to go with that dress, don't you think?" Maria said.

"I agree," she replied. "Could you find her a pair of five inch heels and see how she goes with them," she said to the saleswoman.

"Certainly madam." She found a pair of black leather stilettos, very pointy with a tiny black bow just behind the toe.

"I'll try these on you Miss," she said to, kneeling down. She fitted the shoes to my feet, they were a perfect fit, a size seven which was my normal shoe size.

"Miss, why don't you try walking in them, see how they feel."

I stood up and it was lucky that Ruth and Maria were stood either side of me. They were expecting me to have difficulty and they weren't wrong. I took a step and nearly went flying, the shoes were so difficult and uncomfortable to walk in.

"You need to take short, careful steps if you're not used to them, Miss," the saleswoman said.

I thanked her and tried again. Sure enough, by taking short steps, initially just a few inches at a time, I was able to quickly get used to walking in them and found that after a few minutes I was able to walk almost normally.

Both Ruth and Maria were delighted. "They're absolutely gorgeous, Kathy, you'll have to take them," Ruth said.

I wasn't entirely sure that I would be able to walk in them very far, but both girls swept over my objections.

"You need to look really pretty for a night out, Kathy," Maria said. "Why don't you keep them on and you can practice walking in them while we're looking round the town. That way you'll be used to them for the evening."

"That's a good idea, Maria," Ruth said. "Yes, keep the shoes on, Kathy, you can just change out of your little black dress and put your skirt and blouse back on."

They found the changing room and I changed out of my little black dress and put my tartan miniskirt and school blouse back on. I slipped back into the high-heeled shoes and tottered back out to see the girls.

"I'm not sure if I'll manage walking in these," I moaned. "I feel that I have to spend all of my time concentrating on staying upright."

"All girls have to get used to that," Ruth said. "After a while, you won't even remember you're wearing them. You probably don't realize that with your corset laced tighter, wearing the high-heeled shoes forces you to walk with something of a sexy wiggle." She grinned, "I reckon you'll have all the boys after you if you're not careful."

"I hope not," I said.

I thought I heard one of them mutter, 'we'll see,' but maybe I was wrong.

CHAPTER 4

When we finally got home my feet were killing me, tottering round the city in five inch heels was not the most relaxing way to walk. They laughed off my discomfort as something that all girls experienced.

"Kathy, take a shower and we'll give you a hand to get ready to go out," Ruth said.

I was already used to doing what they told me, the business of being a girl was something I was getting used to and even enjoying, but I still had a lot to learn. When I came out of the shower and went into my bedroom, they were both waiting for me. I had my pink satin dressing gown on so I wasn't embarrassed that Maria was there, but when Ruth told me to strip off it was a different story entirely.

"For Christ's sake, Ruth, you know I can't strip off in front of Maria, she's my sister."

"Look, the sooner you get used to the fact that we are all girls together, the better it will be," Ruth said. "Anyway, I've got something to help you be a little more discreet, a little more girly. Maria, turn your back and I'll help Kathy get this on."

Maria giggled, but turned around. She obviously knew what was coming and had discussed it with Ruth. Without any argument, Ruth just dragged my pretty dressing gown off of me and I stood there naked.

"Right, step into this," she said. I pulled the strange garment up my legs, it was similar to a thong with a pouch for my penis and testicles. She helped me to guide them into it and then fastened the thin straps so that I almost gasped in pain as it dragged my tackle up and between my legs.

"You see, Kathy," Ruth said. "There is the little matter of your male organs, you don't want to show anything like that when you're supposed to be a girl. This little gadget will hold them up high between your legs so that nothing will show through your knickers."

"Christ, Ruth," I said. "It's more uncomfortable than my corset, besides, how can I take a pee when I'm wearing this?"

"It's designed to allow that, Kathy," she replied. Your penis is fitted into a tube with a small hole at the end, so when you need to pee you just sit down and go like any girl."

I wasn't terribly happy about one of the last vestiges of my manhood disappearing up between my legs, but I had to admit it did make a certain sense. I just wished that it wasn't so bloody uncomfortable.

"Right, Maria and I will help you get dressed, you don't need to be embarrassed now, you're just one of us girls. You've got nothing showing," she smiled.

Maria turned around and took a good long look at my crotch, I felt my face beginning to redden.

"Good Lord, Kathy, that looks really good, you're one of us now, you look so female."

"Yes, she does look good," Ruth said. "Let's get her corset on her and we'll make her look even better when we've finished."

I wondered what they meant but I quickly found out. I held up my hands and they pulled the long, heavy corset over my body. I realized that this wasn't my usual corset.

"Ruth, what is this? You bought me a new corset?"

"Yes, dear," she said. "Maria and I wanted you to look especially good for your first night out, so we bought this one for you, it will shape your figure wonderfully. Hang on and we'll get it fastened, you'll see."

They stood behind me and began pulling in the laces, I felt my waist constricting even more than it had before, then they really heaved and I found myself unable to breathe.

"Girls, I can't wear this, it's much too tight, I can't manage it," I said loudly, as I gasped for breath.

"Kathy, you really don't get it. You need this to make your waist sexy and narrow, after a short while you will be used to it and forget you're even wearing it."

I was dubious, but I tried to put the pain and discomfort of the corset to the back of my mind while the girls worked to get me ready. They gave me a pair of black stockings to roll onto my legs, I fastened them to my suspenders. Unlike my usual school stockings these were opaque, very sheer, 15 denier, that showed off my legs to perfection.

"We got you some new panties," Maria smiled. "I bought them, they were my treat for my favorite sister."

She handed me the flimsy black satin panties, they were indeed very sexy and I was astonished at the very attractive female body that was materializing before me. My little black dress did not need any petticoat so I pulled it on. Ruth put a towel around my neck and started on my make up while Maria went to work on my hair.

"I got you some earrings," Ruth said. "The studs you have been wearing for school are fine, but you need something more elegant to go out."

She removed my studs and fastened new dangly earrings to the holes in my ears. They were more than an inch long, I was astonished at the difference they made as I turned my head from side to side and the earrings flashed as they caught the light.

"Kathy, keep your head still," Maria laughed. "I'm trying to make your hair look beautiful."

I kept my head rigid as she worked and Ruth seemed to spend much more time than normal working on my face.

"You should feel really honored, Kathy," Maria said. "It's normally only brides before their wedding that get this kind of personal treatment. I think I'm about done now, Ruth."

"Yes, me too, her makeup looks perfect. Kathy, slip into your high heels and stand up, let's take a look at you."

I wobbled to my feet and stepped over to the mirror. The difference was absolutely astonishing, the 16-year-old schoolgirl had gone completely and instead what stared back at me was a curvy, narrow-waisted and extremely elegant young woman. I must have stood staring at myself for a couple of minutes, suddenly I turned around, and the girls were both laughing.

"Oh yes," Ruth said. "You can't stop admiring yourself in the mirror can you, Kathy? I think we got it right."

I grinned at them, it was true. I was thrilled that they had made me look so good.

"You've done a fabulous job, you two. I can't wait to go out on the town. Thankyou."

"Not so fast, girl," Ruth said. "The surprises haven't finished yet, but while Maria and I are getting ready, you'd better do your nails. You can borrow my bright red nail varnish, you don't need to use clear varnish, that's only for school."

I thanked her again and sat down at the dressing table to start working on my fingernails. I was already quite used to applying clear nail varnish and the red presented no problems. When I had finished, I admired both of my hands, then stood up to look at myself in the mirror again. There was no doubt about it, I looked absolutely gorgeous. I left the bedroom and went downstairs to wait for the girls. I sat reading a girlie magazine that they had bought me, insisting that I needed to do all the things that girls normally did. I was looking at some of the new season's fashions when the girls came down to join me.

"Kathy, you'll need a jacket to go out, Maria said you can borrow this," Ruth said.

She gave me a light cotton jacket in the style of a trench coat, I pulled it on and buttoned it up and admired myself in the mirror.

"Sis, you'll have to stop doing that, you'll become really vain," Maria laughed. "But I have to admit, you've got something to be vain about, Ruth and I would both admit that you are the best looking girl in this room."

"It's true," Ruth said. "You really do look much nicer than either of us. Here, you can borrow my purse, it's plain black and will complement your outfit."

She handed me a small purse with a thin shoulder strap, I hung it on my shoulder and couldn't resist taking yet another peep in the mirror, which caused gales of laughter. But it did look good, the perfect accessory for my dressy outfit.

"Look, Sis," Maria said seriously. "Ruth and I have got another surprise for you, you may not like it but we think it is really important that you go along with it."

They stood looking at me uneasily.

"Come on, tell me what this surprise is," I said to them. "I can't wait, I feel so excited."

It was true, I felt more excited than I had ever felt in my life, I couldn't believe that I would feel like this, that I would enjoy being dressed up as a pretty young woman, even trussed into my painful corset made no difference. I wouldn't let it ruin my evening. Despite the high-heeled shoes that I knew would be agony in a few hours time, I was going to get on with. Kathy Gilmer was going out to enjoy herself!

"There are three of us," Ruth said. "When you go out, it is normal to go in pairs. We were a bit worried about you, it could be a problem if you were approached by a boy who might put you in a very difficult and embarrassing situation. So Maria and I are going together, just as two girlfriends and we've got someone to go with you."

I was surprised, I wondered who it could be. Kaylee?

"We've fixed you up with a date, he's a guy from where I work, his name is Lawrence. He is a really great guy, we're sure you'll love being with him."

I had been on such a high and now I felt the bottom falling out of my world. A guy? Underneath my pretty dress and make up, that is exactly what I was too, a guy, no matter how much I felt like a girl. I felt my anger rising.

"You can't be serious? I can't go out with a guy, that would make me, well, queer."

Ruth was shaking her head. "No, no, not at all. Kathy,

you are a very pretty girl, never mind what nature gave you. You're going out to enjoy this evening as a girl and nothing would be more normal than for you to go with a guy. Besides, I had to tell Lawrence that underneath you used to be a guy yourself, so he knows what you're hiding in your knickers." She smiled broadly. "But he really doesn't mind."

"He doesn't mind?" I asked. "How the hell could he not mind?"

"It's because he's gay, Kathy. Well, maybe not gay exactly, he's kind of bisexual, I think. But he's really looking forward to taking out for the evening."

I wanted to argue, but the doorbell sounded and Maria went to answer it. She showed a guy into the room and I got my first glance at Lawrence. I don't know why, but some kind of a girlie reaction hit me and I looked at him as a potential boyfriend, rather than as an enemy. What I saw was a good looking, slim young man of about 20. He was dressed quite trendily in jeans and an Armani T-shirt. Over that he was wearing an expensive leather jacket. His hair was quite long, almost to his shoulders, combed in a sort of surfer style which suited his hair color, a light and dark streaked effect as if he had been surfboarding on a Californian beach for several months. His eyes were dark brown and I could see that he was looking me up and down in the same way that I was looking at him. I could see that he liked what he saw.

"Hi, I'm Lawrence, you must be Kathy," he said. He came over to me and I held out my hand to shake his.

He stepped past it and gave me a gentle kiss on the cheek.

"Nice to meet you, Kathy, I think we're going to have a good night tonight."

I stared at him, not sure whether to be flattered by his attention to me as an attractive young girl or horrified at the prospect of being kissed by another man. I decided to let it go and just smiled and nodded at him.

"Nice to meet you too, Lawrence," I said. "I'm sure we'll enjoy it."

We left the house and Lawrence had his car parked outside, I was enormously impressed, it was a beautifully restored black vintage Chevvy Impala. He opened the passenger door and pulled the seat forward allowing Maria and Ruth to climb into the back. Then he pushed the seat back and helped me to sit in the passenger seat. He walked around the other side of the car and climbed in, started the engine and drove away. Half an hour later, we were walking around the city centre, enjoying the sights and looking for a bar where we could get our first drink. Lawrence was holding my hand as if I was his girlfriend, I let him to do it, not wanting to cause any kind of a fuss. But I kind of enjoyed it.

I realized that Ruth and Maria had a point about inviting Lawrence along. It was quite obvious that there were so many guys around looking for a date for the night that I would have had to fend them off in droves had I not had a man with me. We sat at a table in a bar chatting happily and I realized that I really was truly happy. I loved looking the way did, so attractive that other men were constantly gazing in my direction, women looked at me with envy in their eyes. Lawrence was really interesting and before long we found ourselves talking about the things that we shared in common. His primary interest was art, a subject that I had enjoyed at school, one of my ambitions was to tour Europe looking at the famous galleries. It turned out that he shared a similar ambition and we chatted away so intensely that the girls had to drag us off to go to the club.

"Come on, you two," Ruth said with a laugh. "You are so into each other that I think we'll have to prize you apart with a crowbar at the end of the night."

We got up and Lawrence took me by the hand and we followed the two girls. I noticed that they were holding hands too, I suppose that girls often did this, I made a note of it. If I was to be a convincing girl holding another girl's hand was perfectly normal. Then again, they did seem to keep looking at each other for long periods. They were so together, so into each other that I began to find it a little peculiar. Still, they were the two people closest to me in my life, had effectively saved my life in fact. I resolved to do my best to be as understanding as I possibly could be towards them. Besides, I had my own problems.

We found a nightclub and went in, Lawrence got us a table and went to get drinks. When he sat down again, he put his arm around me and his face very close to mine.

"Kathy, I'm really glad that Ruth suggested I come along this evening. I hope that I'll be able to see you again when this night is over."

I was stunned. What could I say? It was a very odd situation, yet how could I sit here, a pretty girl with a boy, and effectively tell him to finish up the night and fuck off?

"We'll see how it goes," I replied. "Yes, it would be nice if we could see each other again."

I thought I was pretty safe in saying that. Evidently, he understood that I meant something more, for he pulled my face close to his and kissed me passionately on the lips, the kiss was very erotic, I felt his tongue exploring inside my mouth and his other hand pressed against my back, so that I could not pull away. It was amazing that I enjoyed the kiss, but I felt really guilty at the same time. I noticed Ruth and Maria looking at us, slightly open mouthed but obviously very amused.

"Shall we dance," Lawrence asked me.

I wanted to get away, but I nodded and he led me onto the dance floor. We danced a couple of fast numbers, then the music slowed down and I found myself held in his strong arms, pressed against his body. I was terrified, yet exhilarated. On a more practical note, I had been finding my high heels incredibly painful and it was difficult for me to hold my balance on the dance floor. His holding me did at least give me some support. When the dance ended, he kissed me again, passionately and deeply. We went to sit down and I stared down at the table, not sure what to say, what to do, should I go home, should I tell him to go? I really had no idea, but Ruth could see the dilemma I was in and she leaned over and whispered in my ear,"he is a lovely boy and really fond of you, be nice to him, Kathy. Do it for me."

At the end of the evening Lawrence drove us home, Ruth and Maria went inside the house and once more Lawrence wanted to neck with me on the doorstep. I was still unsure, but I let it happen. I would be able make some firm decisions about the way I wanted things to go with him, for now I just wanted to be inside my own home without any fuss. Eventually he left and I went inside. As I walked in, Ruth and Maria pulled away, they looked incredibly guilty as if they too had been necking. Surely not, I thought? I spent the following day doing my school homework and pressing my clothes ready for the following day. Ruth said that I could keep the trench jacket to wear to school over my blazer, I thanked her and hung it in the wardrobe ready for the following day. The next morning I put on my uniform. Maria and Ruth laced me into my new corset so that I could begin to experience having a much smaller waist.

"If you do need to do anything strenuous like sports, you'll still be able to manage in the corset," Ruth said. "It will obviously make it a little more difficult but you should be able to manage. Women have been managing from long time in garments like that. You won't be able to remove it yourself, of course."

It was on the tip of my tongue to say that if that was

the case why didn't she wear a similar corset, but I kept my mouth shut. I put the jacket on over my blazer and picked up my backpack, said goodbye to the girls and went to catch the school bus. When I got to the bus stop, Kaylee was there with the others, desperate to know what I had been doing on the Saturday night in the nightclub. Apparently I had been seen. I managed to give an innocent explanation, just an evening out with a friend, but they clearly felt that I was some kind of a femme fatale and they grinned and nudged me all the way to school. I couldn't wait for my first real shooting lesson. After lunch, Kaylee and I went to the shooting range and met Miss Johnson who was waiting for us with a pair of handguns.

"These are the same as the guns you tried out last week, girls," she said. "Put on your ear protectors and you can start practicing straight away. Remember to line up the front sight with the back sight, hold it on the target and keep your eyes wide open as you squeeze the trigger. Do not close your eyes, got that?"

We told her we were okay with the shooting technique and took one of the guns each. We stood in an open booth, one for each of us, and I loaded my pistol with bullets. I had six rounds in the magazine and I carefully took aim and fired the first one. I fixed my gaze on the target and fired again, then again, until I had gone through all six rounds. Ms Johnson had given us a box of bullets each, so I reloaded and fired again. Strangely, I found that my excessively tight corset helped me aim the handgun, it kept my body rigid so that I could concentrate on firing. I fired a total of 48 rounds into the target, and then reeled it in. I was pleased. Two of my shots had hit the bull, I was on the way. Look out, thug! Kathy wasn't quite so defenceless now. I persuaded Miss Johnson to let me practice each day in the shooting range, telling her that I would ideally like to become good enough for the Olympics. It was a lie, but I had to have a good enough reason, and after a short while she decided to let me go ahead. Kaylee was not so interested in shooting, so mostly I went there each day on my own. I got better and better each day, more shots went into the bull's eye. Now for the next problem. There was no chance of taking one of the school guns, they were checked and locked away after each session. No, I had to find somewhere where I could buy one.

At the end of the day, Miss Johnson called the cheerleading team together.

"Girls, we need to take more pride in our cheerleading team. In common with some other schools, you are to wear your cheerleading dresses throughout the school day, you work hard to be on the team so wear them as a badge of pride."

The girls shrieked and cheered. It was true, they were much admired and envied around the school. The boys went mad for them, already I could see some of the girls working out which boys they could make a play for in the skimpy little dresses. For me, it was the last thing I needed. Being on the cheerleading team was difficult and uncomfortable in the stiff, tight corset. I couldn't remove it myself, it fastened with the laces at the back, so I changed in a cubicle and didn't shower until I got home. The next morning, Maria and Ruth gaped when I came down to breakfast in my little red cheerleading dress.

"Kathy, that's so pretty," Maria said. "I almost wish I was still at the school. So you've been told to wear them all of the time?"

I nodded

"You should be pleased, it looks lovely," she smiled. But I felt Ruth's eyes on me, they were dancing with merriment. The following weekend they left for Italy, my sister was due back in a week's time. I took the opportunity to change into my slinky black dress after school. I put on my trenchcoat jacket, checked my purse for cash and slung it on my shoulder, and then I went out.

The first gun shop I came to looked extremely smart, perhaps a little too respectable for what I had in mind. I thought it was worth a try. I went inside and stood looking at racks and racks of rifles, shotguns and pistols. A salesman came up to me, a guy who looked to be in his mid-forties, balding.

"Hi," he smiled. "My name is Ben, how can I help you? Are you looking for anything in particular?"

I told him that I had been practicing with a Smith and Wesson .22 pistol in the school shooting range and I wanted to buy my own gun now that I was becoming more proficient. He nodded and went to a display case, unlocked it and pulled out a Smith and Wesson that looked virtually identical to the one I shot with at school.

"Here you are, Miss, I think this might be what you're looking for. It's a nice gun, very suitable for young ladies and it is a very accurate and reliable weapon. Here, would you like to handle it?"

I thanked him and looked at the gun, conscious all the time that his eyes were raking me up and down, assessing every curve, my long dark legs so elegant in the high heels and my luscious, red lips. A Smith and Wesson was exactly what I wanted, the next bit was going to be more difficult. I assumed a sexy pose, jutting out my hip and opening my rich red lips in a gentle smile. I could almost see his knees trembling as he looked at what was on offer before him.

"The thing is, Ben," I said. "My parents are away at the moment, I have ID for myself but I'm sixteen, would that be old enough for me to buy the gun?"

He shook his head, but he was still looking at my body as he said, "I'm really sorry, Miss, but you're not old enough to buy the gun today without your parents being present."

Here goes, I thought. It was time to explore the extent of my power as an attractive young girl over an older man.

"Ben," I said in a low, gentle voice. "I really would like to take the gun away with me today. Is there any way I could persuade you to bend the rules a little? You can see that I'm not someone that's going to use the gun illegally, I really do need to buy one so that I can practice my shooting."

"Well," he said thoughtfully, "the difficulty is that if anyone checks I could get into trouble."

"Look, I really do want to get lots of practice in, I'm planning on trying out for the Olympic team next year."

He looked impressed. "Really?" He said.

"Really," I replied. "Look, Ben, is there anywhere where we can go so that you can give me a private demonstration of the pistol with a view to me buying it today?"

To my utter astonishment I was about to achieve my first victory as a woman. I could see that he was aroused by the attractive young woman stood in front of him, I had doused myself in Ruth's most expensive French perfume and his male hormones were already beginning to overwhelm him.

"Yes, we could do that, we've got a spare shooting range at the side of the building, let's go in there and I'll show you everything in more detail."

I followed him through a door at the side of the shop and we were in a long narrow shooting range, only wide enough to accommodate two shooters. There was a small room at the back of the range, presumably where shooters could sit and wait their turn. The room was furnished with a couch and small coffee table.

"If you would sit on the couch, Miss?" he said to me, "I'll show you where everything is."

"It's Kathy, Kathy Gilmer," I told him. I had already decided to use my real name, once I had used the gun for my intended purpose I planned to ditch it in the sea where it would be lost forever, so I was not overly concerned about it being traced back to me. I realized that I was already beginning to think of myself as Kathy Gilmer, of it being my real name. It was almost as if my previous life was receding into the background. I pushed the thought to one side, I'd worry about it later. If I was honest with myself I would admit that I was having much more fun and leading a far more interesting life as Kathy than I ever had before as Robert. Even going back to school was fun, although I would prefer not to have to wear the cheerleading dress all day and every day, I felt so vulnerable. Ben put the gun on the coffee table and then put one hand behind my shoulders and the other behind my head and pulled me towards him. He kissed me with a savage intensity that took me by surprise. I reminded myself to focus on the mission I was on to stop myself from pulling away with distaste. His tongue explored inside my mouth. I had no choice if I was to achieve what I wanted so I reciprocated, exploring his mouth with my own tongue.

"I was thinking about a blow job, Kathy, you think you could do that?" He asked.

I thought for a moment, it reminded me of the savage thug that was the reason that I was here trying to buy a gun illegally. But I reminded myself that this was something different, this would be my choice to do or not to do. Besides, I had already given one man a blow job, admittedly when he raped me, but I knew what was involved and reckoned that I could manage to do it again.

"Yes, if that's what it takes for you to sell me the gun today, I'll do it for you."

Then I decided to explore my newly found feminine power even more.

"Ben, you're such attractive man, I bet all of the girls go after you," I murmured.

He smiled with pride, "yes, I guess you could say that."

Inside I was laughing, a middle-aged guy who was both bald and boring would be the last person that a girl like me would be interested in. Then I checked again, what was I saying, a girl like me? I put the thought to one side again, I would think about it later.

CHAPTER 5

I unzipped his pants and gently felt inside for his cock, which was already hard and ready for sex. I eased his cock out of his pants and held it in both hands, stroking gently. He began to breathe harder, gasping in short pants as he became more and more aroused. Then I bent down and took his cock in my mouth. It was bad, but not was awful as the brutal rape before. I tried to think of Lawrence, as if I was giving him a blow job and not this shop assistant sleaze ball. I kissed all around his cock, licked it and sucked it, in and out, getting a gentle rhythm going. His hands held my head, as if he was desperate that I would stop. He needn't have worried, I needed that gun, and besides, I wasn't giving this perv a blow job, it was my boyfriend Lawrence. But even as I licked and sucked, my mind was still whirling. I kept thinking of myself as a girl, even enjoying picturing myself as a girl. It would have to stop, this was something temporary and when it was all over I would be able to get out of this uncomfortable corset and crippling high-heeled shoes and put my own clothes back on.

Did I want to do that? I didn't know, the idea of going back to being Robert, a life so dull and boring, did not tempt me so much as the idea of continuing to be the pretty young schoolgirl Kathy, with her school friends and her social life. Even if it did mean wearing that dammed cheerleading dress! I got my mind back to the job in hand, Ben was almost at his peak, sobbing and sighing with the tension of my blowing him. I kept the rhythm going, determined to give him his money's worth and make sure that he didn't go back on his promise to let me have the gun. Finally, I heard him cry out with ecstasy as he came to a climax. Again, he kept hold of my head and forced his cock deeper and deeper down my throat as he spurted, so that the semen trickled down inside me. But it hadn't killed me before, and it wouldn't kill me now, it was just something that we girls had to get used to, I reasoned. There it was again, we girls. What the hell was I going to do when it was time to take back my old life? I decided to worry about it another time.

Ben gave out a final groan and slumped onto the couch. There was a sink in the corner of the room and I got out to rinse out my mouth.

"Kathy, that was absolutely fantastic. You will come

back again, won't you?"

"Ben, of course I'll come back. You're fantastic, a real man. A girl like me doesn't meet many men like you in her lifetime," I told him breathlessly. I admit I really put on the little girl act, dazed by this man's sexual prowess, but I was determined to get what I wanted.

"Don't make it too long then, Kathy," he said. "Come on, do you want to take that gun?"

"I'd love to, Ben. Shall I pay with my Visa card?"

"That would be fine. I can offer you a twenty percent discount as you are about to become a special customer, how is that?" he smiled

"Wonderful," I breathed. We went back into the gun shop and Ben packed the Smith and Wesson in a box.

"I'll throw in a box of ammunition, my compliments," he said.

"You're really very kind," I smiled demurely.

"If you'd like to come and sit at the desk, we'll fill out the paperwork."

We went to his desk and I sat down, careful to keep my legs together and cross one over the other so that the hem of my dress slipped up a little to display the tops of my stockings and a glimpse of suspender. I think he nearly had heart failure, he had to try three times before he managed to fill in the paperwork. Eventually it was done, he handed me the carrier bag with my gun and ammunition and I was ready to go.

"You will come back soon, Kathy," he asked me desperately.

"You bet, Ben," I said to him, I gave him a saucy wink and left the store.

When I got home, I felt powerful, as if I had regained a part of my life, freed myself from some of the terror that had descended upon me and the people I loved. I got out the gun and checked it over, then loaded the magazine with bullets. I snapped on the safety, I was ready. I needed a bigger purse, I couldn't fit the gun into my tiny shoulder purse that Ruth had given. In Ruth's bedroom I found one of her older purses, it was black and quite large. The gun fitted perfectly, I was almost ready to put my plan into action. I looked around the room, Ruth's bedroom? But I had slept in this room too, no, Robert had slept in this room, not Kathy. I put it to the back of my mind, I would think about it later. For the time being, I was a very busy girl with Ruth and Maria away. I had my studies at school to continue with, every night I brought home my home work which I made sure was properly completed. During the school day I worked hard in my lessons, practiced shooting in the range and worked out with the cheerleading squad. I hated my little red dress, I felt so conspicuous in it, all I wanted to do was look like the other girls. I didn't want to stand out, I wanted to be like everybody else, but I had no choice. Lawrence had called around and taken me out for a walk near the harbor a couple of nights ago and I was beginning to grow very fond of him, he was a boy that any girl would be proud to be seen with. And of course, I had my project to work on, my special project. I had started to haunt the area near the offices of the money lender from whom I had borrowed so much money. I made sure that I always wore my little black dress and high-heeled shoes with my black trench jacket so that I didn't remind the thug of the schoolgirl that had been raped. I saw him several times, on one occasion I sat in a coffee bar at a table near him. He was talking to another man that I didn't recognize, but I managed to get his name, it was Joseph. I did my best to follow him several times and find out which routes he took on his way in and out of the money lender's office. At home, I had street maps of the city that I laid out and used to help me with my plans.

The following weekend, on the Saturday morning, I went to a cycle supermarket and bought myself a bicycle. It was a neat machine, a ladies model of course in powder blue with lots of gears. I paid extra to have a wicker basket fixed to the front handlebars so that it had a very old-fashioned, traditional look, very trendy at the moment. I was wearing my school uniform, it would have been impossible to ride the cycle in my short black dress. I rode home and parked it at the back of the house. Then I went back into town and found the shop that sold uniforms for my school. I went in and looked at the girls' hats.

"May I help you, Miss," a woman said to me.

I gave her a bright smile and said, "I am a student at the high school, I would like to buy myself a hat to go with my uniform."

She looked a little surprised. "I'd be happy to sell you one, but not many of the girls wear them these days. Are you sure that's what you want?"

"Oh yes, my parents want me to have one for my official school photograph, so they sent me here to buy one."

"Very well, let's try one on you for size."

She brought out the school uniform hat, a cross between a beret and a bonnet, and tried one on my head. It was a little sloppy so she tried the next size down and it fitted perfectly."

I said I would take it and she wrapped it and I went home. I was almost ready to put my plan into action. I brought my cycle into the house, put on my new school hat and looked at myself in the mirror. There was absolutely no doubt, I looked the absolute picture of innocence. I could be any schoolgirl who was cycling home on her powder blue cycle, wearing her school uniform and her dainty little hat. I decided that on the following Monday, just after six o'clock when everything was busy, I would put my plan into action. Then the phone rang, it was Maria.

"I wanted to find out how you were doing, Kathy," she said.

"I'm fine, how is it in Italy?" I asked her.

"That's what I wanted to talk to about," she replied. "It's really wonderful here, Ruth is working really hard and I'm spending lots of time seeing the sights. I talked to Ruth and I decided to stay for an extra week, she said she didn't mind provided that you were okay. What do you think, Sis,?"

It was perfect, I needed a little more time to settle some affairs. I told her it was no problem and she promised to give me a call during the week. I put the phone down and it rang again almost straight away. It was Lawrence

"Kathy, I wasn't sure if you would be home," he said. "I wondered if you are doing anything this evening."

For some reason I felt utterly daring, perhaps it was the enormity of what I was planning, perhaps it was knowing that I had a handgun and ammunition hidden in my black purse, or perhaps it was me enjoying my life as a pretty girl and wanting to see her boyfriend.

"I'm not doing anything this evening, Lawrence," I replied. "Why don't you come round, maybe I could do you something to eat."

There was a silence from moment. Then he said, "Kathy I'd like nothing better than that. Has Maria come back yet?"

I told him about my conversation with my sister. "It's nice that she is having a good time," he said. I suspected that he felt it was even nicer that we would have the house to ourselves tonight, but perhaps I was wrong. He agreed to be around at eight o'clock that evening, so when I put down the phone I immediately put on my apron and started cleaning the house, which I had somewhat neglected over the past few days of frantic activity. When I was satisfied I went to the local store and bought some food for the evening, steaks, salads and oven ready fries. I carried everything home and put the shopping in the kitchen, then went upstairs to start getting ready. Since Ruth and Maria had been away, I had been forced to fall back on my first corset, which laced at the back and fastened at the front with hooks and eyes. I was disappointed that I wouldn't be able to wear my new corset which dragged my waist in to such a small size, but when I came out of the shower I adjusted the laces on the older corset and put it on, finding that with a huge struggle I could just about fasten the hooks and eyes, provided that I stopped breathing temporarily. I looked in the mirror, I was so pleased that I had managed to pull in my waist so much, almost as much as with the other corset. I put the rest of my clothes on, my little black dress, knowing that he liked me in it. It was the nicest dress I had to wear, and my black stiletto shoes.

In the kitchen, I put my apron on and started preparing the meal. It was nearly eight o'clock by the time I had everything ready, the table beautifully laid, a bottle of wine chilling in the icebox and the steaks sizzling merrily on the grill. The doorbell rang and I let Lawrence in, God, he was handsome. He gave me a huge kiss and we walked into my sitting room hand-in-hand.

"I'm glad you could make it," I said to him.

"I wouldn't have missed this for anything," he smiled.

I served the meal and we chatted while we ate the steaks and sipped at the wine. Afterwards, we went to sit on the couch and watch a movie on our cable TV.

Almost immediately, Lawrence had his hands all over me and I felt so warm, so aroused, so full of a new feeling that I couldn't describe.

"Kathy, I want to make love to you, I don't believe I've ever felt so close to anyone, girl or boy, as I have to you," he said.

"But, Lawrence, you know it's not as simple as that," I replied.

"Of course I know, Kathy, but you know there are ways. I promise you, I only think of you as an extremely attractive girl. If I make love to you, that is what will be in my mind."

I looked into his eyes and saw the depth of sincerity in them.

"We'd better go up to my bedroom," I said to him.

I took him by the hand and we went upstairs to the bedroom, where he stripped me down to my corset.

"Lawrence, I'd like to keep my corset on," I said to him. "It won't stop you doing anything with me, but it makes me feel more like a girl. Is that okay?"

"It's absolutely perfect," he replied. Then, dressed only in my corset, with my manhood concealed in the device that Ruth had fitted on me, I returned the compliment to Lawrence and took all of his clothes off until he was completely naked. I knew that there was one thing I could do for him. I pushed him to the bed and he lay on his back, then I bent down and took his cock in my mouth and gently began sucking him. He moaned with pleasure, the utter pleasure of being with someone that you are very fond of. I gently licked and sucked around the tip of him, all the time my hands were stroking his body, feeling his wonderful face and sliding down his stomach and into his groin where I was able to cup his testicles and stroke them, exciting him even more. Eventually, he could stand it no more.

"Kathy, have you got any lubricant?"

"I think that Ruth keeps some in her bedside cabinet," I replied. "I'll go and get some."

I ran into Ruth's bedroom and found the jelly and took it back to Lawrence, knowing what he was planning. I felt a warm sense of love and a special excitement, it was an emotion that was totally alien to me. He took the jelly, smeared some on his finger and gently, sensuously, pushed it inside my ass, coating the lining of my anus with the slippery gel. He found my prostate and stroked it, sending me into paroxysms of pleasure.

"Lawrence, fuck me, please, give it to me," I gasped.

He pushed me onto my stomach, spread my legs wide and I felt a burning sensation as his cock, already damp with the moisture from my mouth, slid easily into my lubricated hole. It was an amazing and incredible feeling. I was desperate, of course, to seek my own sexual orgasm, but the strap that fastened my manhood between my legs held my cock so tightly that it was impossible for it to become erect. I realized that I would have to take my pleasure in other ways, and indeed Lawrence was a very expert lover, so expert that he found every erogenous zone inside and outside my hole so that the whole of my body tingled with excitement and joy. I wanted the experience to go on forever, the feeling I had for this boy must have been something very close to love. He was my first real partner in my new life as a girl. I surrendered myself to the heat and passion of the moment until eventually I heard him begin to groan with pleasure as he came to a climax. Then he surged inside me, his cock growing even bigger and I felt his semen squirting up into me as he spurted, again and again. We stayed still for a few minutes, finally he relaxed and came out of me, it was over.

Lawrence slept with me that night, in the morning I put on my pink satin dressing gown and went down to make breakfast. When he came down, he smiled and kissed me and sat down to eat his eggs and toast. I spent most of that Sunday relaxing and dreamily thinking about the boy who had become my lover. Eventually, he had to go home and I saw him off at the door with a feeling of sadness inside me. When he had gone, I was still unable to work out the strange feelings that I felt while he was fucking me. I knew that inside I was a boy, yet equally I knew that I had begun to change, to become more of a girl than a boy. I looked like a girl, indeed, people said I was a very pretty girl, and as a girl I seemed to be making much more of a success of my life than I ever had as a boy. However, there was a dark cloud that loomed on the horizon, one that tomorrow night I had to deal with.

The next day, Monday, I was back in school. The day

seemed to drag on endlessly, lesson after lesson, shooting practice, cheerleading squad, my friends chatting to me over dinner and wondering why I was so distracted. I went into the toilets and redid my hair, taking trouble to make sure my plaits were exactly right. When I came out, Kaylee was startled.

"Jesus, Kathy, what have you done? Your hair looked lovely with those long, tiny plaits. Now you've put it into two big plaits, with those ribbons at the end, you look like a little girl."

"I just fancied a change, that's all," I told her.

"Well, ok, but think about changing back to the way it was," she said. "You go around like that and they'll put you back in junior school."

I was pleased, the effect was exactly what I wanted. The afternoon passed as slowly as the morning, with more cheerleading practice. Then the bell rang and it was time to go home. At home, I took extra care to get everything ready. I was too excited to eat. I took off my cheerleading dress and put on my school uniform, complete with tartan mini-skirt. I pulled on my blazer and fastened the buttons, so that it looked quite prim and correct. Then the hat, I picked it up and fastened it on my head. I looked in the mirror, perfect, a dainty little bonnet that reinforced what I actually was - a regular schoolgirl. I picked up my black purse and checked the gun, it was ready to fire. I slipped the safety to the off position and placed it carefully back into the purse.

CHAPTER 6

I was ready. I left the house, wheeled my cycle out to the road and cycled away. I must have been a pleasant sight as I rode along, the pretty young schoolgirl on the powder blue cycle, wearing my school blazer and bonnet, because I noticed several people smile in my direction. I carried on into town and stopped a block away from the money lender's office. There I waited in a narrow alley, screened from the road, and let the air out of my back tire. Then I got the pump and started to pump air back in.

I needed a good reason to be waiting in this spot, a flat tire was perfect. I had to fend off three offers of help from men, two old, one of them young, who wanted to do the pumping for me. Then I saw him emerge from the office, Joseph, looking huge and menacing as usual. I knew that he would come past this alley, so I pushed my cycle behind some dustbins to hide while he went by. I already knew his appetite for young girls in school uniform. The thug walked quickly on his way to the coffee bar, I knew his route exactly. I gave him a good start, then climbed onto my cycle and followed. A few yards in from of him was my destination, a wide gap between two huge restaurant dustbins. I put on some speed and rode past him, then swerved into the gap and propped my cycle against a bin. I got out my Smith and Wesson, double checked that the safety was off, and then held it ready. I had expected to be shaking at this point, but I was ice cool. The thug was a piece of refuse that I needed to clear off of the streets so that no other girls were raped. He arrived adjacent to the bins and saw me standing between them. He looked surprised, then pleased when he saw that it was his favorite dish, a uniformed schoolgirl. He hadn't noticed the gun.

"Hi, darling," he started to speak. "You need me to help you with something?"

"Hi, Joseph," I said, smiling sweetly at him. "I'm the girl you raped a while back, remember?"

He looked puzzled, then remembered.

"Oh, yes, I remember, the gambling debt. Back for more, are you, sweetie? Let's see what else you've got."

"Oh, don't worry, you will," I smiled. He looked puzzled again until I lifted up the gun. I took aim, he tried to grab for the gun but I was too fast for him. The practice paid off, I fired four shots into the area around his heart. At first he looked shocked. Then, as blood spurted out of his chest, his eyes rolled and he fell over, giving a last, dying breath. The .22 was quiet as handguns go, but four shots still make a noise.

I put the gun into my purse, put the purse into my wicker basket and backed my cycle out from behind the bins, away from the body. Then I simply climbed on and rode away. As I pedaled, I could hear a woman screaming and a siren wailing in the distance. I took no notice as I headed for the Charles River. I rode out onto a bridge and propped up my cycle while I stood, apparently looking across the city. When no-one was near, I simply dropped the handbag into the deep river. I had weighted it with some rocks so that together with the pistol and ammunition, it plunged out of sight, straight to the bottom.

I rode slowly home. When I got indoors, I felt faint. I turned on the TV. The slaying of a known muscleman for a notorious money lender was headline news. Even better, when the police searched the body, they found a notebook in his pocket with extensive records of illegal loan sharking, money laundering, protection rackets and prostitution. The money lender was arrested and everything pointed to him going away for a very long time. Nobody had noticed the killer, they reported seeing only a few innocent bystanders going past.

One person said that he saw an old lady walking her dog and a schoolgirl in uniform riding her cycle home from school, but the police knew that they would have to look somewhere else for the killer. I opened a bottle of wine to celebrate my freedom. I should really drink alcohol at my age, sixteen, but what the hell, I deserved it. Wait a minute, was I sixteen? No, of course not, I was twenty, no, that was Robert. Damn, who the hell was I?

The following evening I phoned Lawrence and asked him to call around.

"Problems?" he asked me.

"I just need to talk, Lawrence, I'm really confused right now."

"No worries, Kathy, I'll call round later."

He put the phone down and I sat and read a magazine, Cosmopolitan. There were some good articles, I had bought it during the week on Kaylee's recommendation. I thought about Ruth and Maria, and then had an idea. I looked in my notebook and found the telephone number of the apartment Ruth had rented in Milan, Italy, then dialed the number.

"Kathy, how nice to hear from you," Ruth said. "Is everything ok?"

"Not really, Ruth," I said.

"You're not ill are you?" She had a panicky note in her voice."

I told her I was fine and explained that the money lending nightmare seemed to be over with the death of the collector and arrest of the owner of the company. She was surprised, unable to frame an answer.

"Kathy, that's wonderful, well, that's good. Er, what are your plans now?"

There was a silence while I thought about her

question. Then she spoke again.

"I mean, you are going to finish school, Kathy? You're not going to do anything different, for now?"

She sounded concerned, but I had already worked out why.

"You don't need to worry, Ruth. I think I understand how close you are to Maria. You're worried that Robert will want to resurface and jump back into your bed, aren't you?"

She was shocked that I had worked it out. "So you know about us, that we have become lovers?"

"I knew, at least, I'd worked it out. Ruth, I won't stand in your way."

"I don't understand, Kathy. What's going on, why aren't you bringing Robert back? Is something else wrong?"

"That's the problem," I replied. "Nothing is wrong. I feel that I've not only changed my appearance to look exactly like Kathy Gilmer, I have become Kathy Gilmer. It's who I am. Ruth, I honestly don't know what to do now. All I do know is that I love being who I am, I don't want it to change."

"Jesus Christ, Kathy, that is a real blockbuster. I don't know what to say. So you'll be staying on at school."

"Yes, and the other things, my friends, my sports, it's what I'm happy doing."

"Kathy, have you got someone in your life? Is it Lawrence?"

"We do see a lot of each other. But that's not an issue,

the thing is, I'm unsure about everything, about myself. I don't know what to do. I'm not technically a girl, but I feel like Kathy Gilmer, it's who I am. Technically I'm a guy, but how can that be, when inside I know that I'm really Kathy Gilmer? What's happening to me, Ruth? And what do we do? Remember, we're still married."

"There's only one thing to do, Kathy. Stay as you are for now and think long and hard. Most important is to talk to Lawrence. Does he like you as a girl, or as a boy? I thought he was gay?"

I told her that we had discussed it, Lawrence had fallen for a girl named Kathy. Not a boy, Robert.

"Talk to him, Kathy. Maria will be home at the end of the week, so you can chat to your twin sister," she laughed.

We said goodbye and I was left to my own thoughts. Lawrence arrived and I cooked him supper, then we sat on the couch and watched a film on TV, just like any normal boy and girl. Weren't we a normal boy and girl? Lawrence had thought he was gay, but liked me as a girl. I was a guy, yet a girl called Kathy with a life at the local high school.

He kissed me deeply, lovingly. "Kathy, I've got something of a secret to tell you?"

"Yes, what is it?"

He hesitated, and then plunged in. "Kathy, I'm in love with you. I know that I thought I was gay, and I know that you are not fully a girl, but it doesn't matter, I'm in love with Kathy Gilmer, the 16 year old schoolgirl."

He kissed me, a kiss so powerful and strong that I thought I would stop breathing.

"Did I hear you correctly, Lawrence, did you use the word love?"

He nodded. "That's right, it's the way I feel, Kathy. Whatever the future holds for me, I want it to be with you."

He held me tightly, I could feel that it was more than his emotions that were getting stronger. I led Lawrence to my bedroom.

"Let me take off your clothes," I said to him. "Just stand there and allow me to pleasure you, my darling."

I slowly, sensuously, removed his clothes, one garment at a time. As I did, I kissed him, first on the lips, then on every part of his body that was bared. Finally he stood naked and I gently pushed him on to the bed. I bent down and licked the end of his penis, smiling as he shivered with pure, animal arousal. Then I sucked him gently, feeling his cock grow larger and larger.

"Lawrence, how can I make it really perfect for you?" I asked.

He grinned. "Kathy, you know what I would really like?"

I shook my head.

"I'd like to screw you in that schoolgirl uniform. You know those short, tartan skirts drive the guys wild? Don't undress, keep it all on and come to bed, I want to ravage my gorgeous little schoolgirl the way she looks now."

I joined him on the bed, and his hand slid under my skirt, inside my knickers and felt my ass. I kissed him some more, touching him, enjoying the taste and smell of my lover, everything about him was so perfect. Then he pulled down my knickers, unable to wait any longer.

"We'll have to do something about your corset, Kathy, it does make it a bit difficult getting to your ass, you know."

"It makes me look very girly, Lawrence, that's why I wear it. You wanted me to come to bed fully dressed, remember?" I smiled. "Next time, I'll take it off just for you."

"Great, I'd like that." He managed to circumvent my corset, his finger probed into my anus, lubricating me, exciting me, then he pushed his cock all the way in and I felt the exciting, hard fullness of him inside me. His hands were caressing my body, his cock pumped in and out and I felt it rubbing inside my ass. When it hit the more sensitive parts the waves of pleasure swept through me in a torrent. He almost came, forcing in, harder and harder.

"Lawrence, stop, I don't want it to end yet," I murmured.

He pulled out of me. "What's up, Kathy?"

"What's up is I don't want it to finish yet. Lie down and let me play with you."

He lay on his back and I went back down on him, teasing his cock, massaging his balls and doing everything short of bringing him to a climax. He groaned and protested, but I would not let him come. Finally, I realized that he was in agony, desperate for orgasm, so I relented.

"Lawrence, fuck me, put your cock back inside me and give me everything you've got," I begged him.

His cock rammed into me, urgent, desperate, and he pumped hard, in and out, sighing with pleasure. My prostate was constantly being rubbed by his organ and I felt myself coming to my own, rather different orgasm, it was really strange. Then he climaxed, whooping with glee as his semen squirted into me, again and again, so that my ass felt totally full of him. We lay there, quiet, enjoying the peace and release of sex with the one you love. He got off of the bed.

"Kathy, can I stay the night? I can leave early in the morning, but I want to be with you. Come downstairs first, I want you to tell me what the problem is, why you called me tonight.

He put his clothes back on and we went downstairs and sat on the couch.

"The problem is, Lawrence, I just don't know who I am. You know how much I feel for you, yet not long ago I was an ordinary married man, although perhaps not a very successful one. I've never been so happy since I became Kathy Gilmer, I feel like I've only just been born and Robert Gilmer is a distant memory that's a long way away. At the same time, I feel that I am a bit of a fraud. I attend school as a girl, go to classes and dance around with the cheerleading team in my little red dress, but if they knew what was hidden inside my knickers it would be a different story. I want to be Kathy Gilmer, I feel that I am Kathy Gilmer, yet I'm not her in fact. What should I do? Should I go back and find Robert again?"

"I see," he said. "I've already told you that my feelings for you are as Kathy."

"Yes, but that's just the tartan miniskirt that turns you on, isn't it?" I smiled.

"Be serious, Kathy," he said. "What I mean is, you know that when I was first introduced to you by Ruth I knew that inside you were a guy, and when I came to the door that night I was expecting to see somebody that looked like a man, although dressed in girl's clothes. I saw you and fell for you straight away, but not because I saw a guy, it was because I saw a girl."

"And if Robert came back, what then?"

"I honestly don't know, Kathy. I never knew Robert and don't know if I would like him or not. I wish I could help you more, but I'm trying to be honest."

"I don't think that Robert will be coming back, how could he, I'm Kathy? I always want to be Kathy, or at least I think I do. But the problem is that I don't know where I fit in. I'm neither one thing nor the other, not fully, anyway."

He went quiet, unable to find an answer.

"Let's watch some TV," I said, turning on the cable channels. We browsed through and eventually came to a cabaret show called the Girlyboys. They were famous, beautiful young boys from Thailand and other parts of

Southeast Asia who grew beautiful breasts, but were still real boys, they had male penises and testicles. Like me, except that I didn't have beautiful breasts. Sadly.

"That's exactly what I mean," I said to Lawrence. "Those people are just like me, they're not real women and not real men. They're something in between, except for those gorgeous tits."

He watched fascinated at the beautiful young 'women' dancing on a stage.

"Perhaps that's what you are, Kathy. Perhaps you were intended to be a Girlyboy."

"Oh God, Lawrence, I don't think I'd have the guts to do that. Besides, how on earth do they get such beautiful breasts, do you think they use surgery?"

He looked closely at their breasts, too closely, I thought with a flash of jealousy.

"I don't know, it's probably a combination of surgery and hormone tablets. Why, are you thinking about getting yourself a nice pair of tits?"

"Would you like me to?" I asked him. His bright smile gave me the answer I needed. We slept together in my single bed, in the morning he left early and went to work. I got myself ready and went to school. On the Thursday, Maria arrived home and we hugged each other, happy to be reunited.

"How you feel, Sis, had any more thoughts?" she asked me.

I told her the way things were and then about seeing the Girlyboys on television.

She listened, fascinated with everything I had found out about them since I saw the show.

"Is that what you're thinking about? Surgery and hormone tablets so that you can have a pair of female breasts?"

"It's a thought," I replied. "At least I wouldn't be quite such a fraud as I am at the moment."

"You're not a fraud," she said hotly. "You are the girl that you feel inside. You know that there is surgery available if you feel that deep down you really are a girl and want to become a girl in every way?"

I told her that of course I had heard of it, but the prospect was terrifying. At the same time, the prospect of carrying on in my sexual limbo was equally distasteful. I changed the subject to her and Ruth.

"How are things between you and Ruth?" I asked.

She looked at me shamefaced and finally admitted that the two of them were engaged in a full-blown lesbian relationship.

"Are you in love?" I asked. She nodded in reply, "yes, I'm afraid we are, Kathy."

"Well at least that ties one thing up, Robert's marriage to Ruth is in the past."

The following morning I got dressed and went to school as usual. When I got home, Maria had news for me.

"Kathy, I've fixed up something of a surprise. We're going out tonight, we need to get going now."

"Where are we going?" I asked her.

"You remember those Girlyboys? I contacted loads of people today and found that they are in New York at the moment. I spoke to their manager and told him all about you and they have agreed that we can go and visit them and you can talk to them and discuss the way you feel. They said they would do everything to help."

"That's great," I said. "Thanks Maria that's really kind, I'd love to talk to them, it seems they have the same sort of problems as I do. You're not expecting me to join them, though, are you?"

She laughed. "No, I don't think that would be a good idea."

CHAPTER 7

We managed to get the short flight to New York, it was late evening by the time we arrived. The Girlyboys were performing in a local hotel and we sat in the bar watching their show. They were even more beautiful in the flesh than they had been on the television screen. All of them had tits that any girl would be proud to call hers. After the show, they came into the bar for a drink and we found a table where we sat around chatting.

It seemed that their problems were very similar to mine, they had been brought up as boys and for various reasons had been introduced to dressing as girls and found that it fitted their personality, their psyche, more than being a boy had. I was never quite sure of their sexuality, not that it made any difference. The one glaring fact that stared me in the face was that they were so confident in who they were. It was like they were a third gender. I was really astonished when they told me about a group of guys in South America, in Mexico, who claimed to belong to a third gender. These people were called Muxes, a beautiful Girlyboy who said her name was Mai, told me. They were female-looking men who dress and live as women. As many as six percent of men in the Zapotec community were reported to be Muxe. There were other Zapotec communities with similar third gender roles, including a group called the Bizaah.

Apparently the three gender system predated Spanish colonization, although the Muxe's dressing as women was fairly recent, beginning in the 1950s and strongly gaining in popularity. Within the Zapotec culture, there were different opinions about their social status, Mai said. Muxe's in village communities were not generally disparaged, although in larger towns they did face some discrimination, especially from typical macho Mexican men. Muxe's generally belonged to the poorer classes of society, because same-sex activities in wealthier communities were more likely to follow the western gay, bisexual and transgender route. Those individuals are also more likely to remain in the closet. In the poorer communities, such as the Zapotec culture, the idea of choosing gender or of sexual orientation seemed silly to them, like suggesting that you can choose your skin color. They believed that most people's gender was something God had given them, whether man, woman, or Muxe. Because of this, Muxe men were not referred to as homosexuals but constituted a separate category. People saw them as having the physical bodies of men but different outlooks, skills and emotions from most men. Some considered that they combined some parts of men and some of women.

It was a fascinating story. Mai chatted on, she was both beautiful and very good company. Maria was talking to another Girlyboy named Durudee, hanging on to her every word, looking fascinated at every word she spoke. Later, I looked around and they had disappeared.

"Kathy, why don't we go up to our suite and we can continue this conversation, the bar is due to close soon," Mai said.

I thanked her, she took my hand and we walked over to the elevator, two pretty girls, friends. We reached the suite and sat on the couch. Mai told me of her long, hard struggle to become successful in Thailand until the Girlyboys became well known. She was still holding my hand, her perfume powerful, spicy and strange, I felt overcome with her beauty, her hypnotic, gentle voice, the touch of her soft skin. She leaned over and kissed me, an amazing kiss that sent shock waves of pleasure rolling through my body. She reached under my skirt with one hand, the other held my head firmly, so that my lips were glued to hers. I didn't object, it was a sensation that was pure delight. She got up and let me into her bedroom, pushed me onto the bed and removed my dress. Her eyes widened when she saw my corset.

"Why do you wear such a heavy corset?" she asked

me. I told her how much I enjoyed having a small waist. She looked at my body, "Kathy, it certainly does look good on you, you look so, girly," she said, and laughed.

She got up, surprising me. "I want to give you a gift, Kathy."

She rummaged in her travel case and came out with my 'gift', a dildo of enormous proportions.

"If you are to be a girl, you need to know how to pleasure yourself as a girl, Kathy."

"Don't you have a cock, Mai?" I asked her. "Why the dildo?"

"I am not proud of my male bits, that's why I use this," she said. "Let me show you."

She pulled down my knickers and turned me over. Then she lubricated the dildo herself, licking and sucking it in such an erotic way that I felt myself becoming enormously aroused. She climbed on the bed and spread my legs.

"Do you want this, Kathy?"

"Yes, please," I breathed.

She pushed it into me, gently, and I felt it probing my ass, deeper, deeper, until I started to panic that I would not be able to accept it all. She started to twist and turn it, unerringly finding my erogenous zones. It was so much bigger, better, more pleasurable than even Lawrence had been when he fucked me. She had an instinct for what would give me the greatest turn on. My cock was firmly trapped in its strap, but it didn't matter, something was churning inside me, like I had felt with Lawrence, but this was different. Mai had a technique that was so experienced, so powerful, that I felt myself slipping away into a different place, a sexual nirvana. Then I came, a rippling, pulsing feeling that surged through my body. Yet, I realized, it was not from my cock. It was something else, something inside me.

"You see," she smiled. "That is why we use a dildo. When you leave, you can take this one with you." She smiled. "I've got some spares to take with me. Kathy, you asked about my penis. Part of being a Girlyboy is having a penis, look."

She pulled down her panties and her cock leapt out. I was startled, it was so at odds with her beauty and grace.

"I can see from your expression that you find it strange, perhaps ugly" she said. "Think about it. I wish I didn't need it."

I found out that Maria had spent time in bed with her Girlyboy, Durudee. I wanted to ask her about it, but she was my sister, I decided not to pry. But I did think about what Mai had said. When I got home, I carried on with my schoolwork, my sports activities, the shooting, seeing Lawrence three times a week, or as often as school would allow. Ruth came home, much to Maria's joy. I invited Lawrence to the house for dinner the following evening to celebrate. I got home from school and looked in the mirror, long and hard. I liked what I saw, liked it a lot. The three of them sat waiting at the table when I went downstairs.

"Hi," I said, smiling to them. "I'm Kathy. Robert is never coming home, ever. I'm going to finish school and then I'll be signing up for surgery. I'm a girl and that's all I ever want to be.

Ruth frowned. "Kathy, I started all this off, do you blame me, or Maria?"

"No," I replied. "You know I talked to you about meeting the girl of my dreams?"

She nodded, yes, I do remember."

"Right," I said, "I've met her and I've become her."

"We're all pleased for you," Maria said. "I've got something for you. I won't go into technicalities, but Kathy's birth certificate and documentation is all yours now. So look, Sis, this is who you are and always will be. It's yours."

She handed me the birth certificate with my name on it. I thanked her. She drew me to one side and whispered.

"I just wanted to apologize, you didn't mind me borrowing your dildo occasionally, did you?"

I shook my head. "No worries, Sis."